GOODBYE
MR. POLITICIAN
and
AFRICAN
CELEBRATION

GOODBYE
MR. POLITICIAN
—and—
AFRICAN
CELEBRATION

STEPHEN KWAME MENDS

Goodbye Mr. Politician and African Celebration

iUniverse books may be ordered through booksellers or by contacting:

iUniverse
1663 Liberty Drive
Bloomington, IN 47403
www.iuniverse.com
1-800-Authors (1-800-288-4677)

ISBN: 978-1-4759-0586-1 (sc)
ISBN: 978-1-4759-0587-8 (e)

Print information available on the last page.

iUniverse rev. date: 03/27/2017

DEDICATION

This book is dedicated to my loving wife Irene Abeh Afriyie Mends,
my friends Silas Obadiah (M.A. Brown University), Eli Agbenya (M.A.
Rhode Island College)
and my secretary Mary Allcock.

SYNOPSIS OF GOODBYE MR. POLITICIAN

BY STEPHEN KWAME MENDS

This is a simple but perennially recurring African story which must be read by women of all walks of life who have been cheated on or raped by chauvinistic men. It has contemporary relevance even in America.

When you look at Hilary Clinton, Elizabeth Edwards (may her soul rest in peace), Sandra Bullock, O.J. Simpson's wife (may she rest in peace), Scott Peterson's wife (may she rest in peace), Oprah Winfrey, Maya Angelou, Elin Woods Nordegren, Maria Shriver, and many others who are not as famous, you will see that cheating, rape, molestation, abuse and disrespect still rages in this God's country. Sex must be sacrosant.

I am always drawn to a woman because she has some compassionate wisdom and tenderness which I first found in my mother and subsequently several other women. My mother is a woman, my sisters are women and just as I hate my female relatives to be subjected to shame, disrespect, bias, sexual violence, domestic violence and painful divorce, so do I not want any female go through these.

Most men are sexual aggressors. However, to me, the only sexual activity that doesn't come with guilt is the one between the legal union of two people. Sex in the unmarried union, whether in the Western Type of dating, rape or molestation always comes with guilt and consequences. No wonder there are so many failed marriages and broken homes.

For us humans, everything we do in truth, honesty, compassion, kindness and good morality make us the genuine Homo sapiens that we should be.

These days we think that adultery, fornication, serial marriages, and war are right. I think that maybe God's commandments (I have no problems with them) are obsolete because there seems to be a New World Order and we should pray to Him to bring new ones to reflect all our follies. As I have always realized, Homo sapiens should actually be called Homo stultus because we appear to be more foolish, wicked, and unforgiving than even animals.

Without women the continuity of humankind will be put on hold. Women suffer. Mary suffered a lot to see her son crucified by sinful men and that is enough.

This is the tragic story of Agya Sei, a bigamist and a politician. It is an election year in the U.S.A. and Ghana. The book explores the idea of open marriage, and polygamy and involves the eternal themes of power and the corruption of the individual (and a society) enthralled with its attainment. It is a colorful, fluid and ultimately engaging story.

GOODBYE MR. POLITICIAN

BY STEPHEN KWAME

Agya Sei was quite popular in his village. Although a very hard worker, he had never seen the fruits of his labor displayed in extravagance yet. However, his deepest hopes came into fruition when the Democratic Party, of which he was a member, succeeded in getting the people of his constituency to vote for him to be a member of parliament.

Throughout his political campaigning, two main things had occupied his mind. One, of course, was the obvious—victory. The other too, which to him, was equally important and carried the same weight as victory was success in winning the very young, very beautiful and secondary school literate—one of the only few girls who were such endowed. Agya Sei had furtively tried on several occasions to win her but met with dismal failure. This succeeded in giving him a rapid heart anytime he thought about it. He feared, perhaps, that these previous secret attempts at winning her had been broadcast about and that all the youth in the village had got to know about it. No wonder the village beauty had been consciously avoiding him.

His shame was profound in this respect but he refused to accept it. No matter how much the power of ridicule seemed to defeat him, he still maintained his own good sense. Persistence, he knew too well, had fulfilled many cherished hopes for many men and women of strong faith. Therefore, after the political battle had been won, if he had to go

1

on his knees or go around the world to do it, he was still prepared to do them to win his dream girl.

Agya Sei knew certainly well that to get the votes of all, mobilization of the youth should feature conspicuously. On previous occasions, he had succeeded in getting them to do communal labor. The young men quite often weeded round the village and right to the stream which was the only source of their drinking water. Out of his own pockets, he had bought palmwine and akpeteshie (moonshine) for the workers, so when he proposed that new latrines should be dug, the young men readily agreed. The village chief himself had endorsed Agya Sei's nomination for all his work in the village. But was Agya Sei's motive for organizing the youth so much single; definitely not because such actions were geared towards seeing more and more of his dream girl. It didn't matter that he himself had a long standing marriage which had seen more happiness than woes. It didn't matter that some of his own children were older than this girl. Much love for this girl which bordered on pure physical lust would be repugnant to his very close friend Akwasi. But Agya Sei had so much confidence in him that he was ready to divulge what was churning up in his mind and weighing him down to this friend. He got up and walked towards where he would find Akwasi. The palmwine bar—This place was for men. More often than not, that was the place for so much political conversation and arguments which embraced the village community and the country as a whole. It was the only place where the daily newspaper, although a day or two old, could be found.

When Agya Sei got there, yes, Akwasi was sitting on one of the reserved seats. Agya Sei's presence caused a stir as everybody wanted to shake his hand and congratulate him. Akwasi quickly made a place for him.

"Good morning Akwasi."

"F-F-F-Fine morning. H-Have a seat."

Akwasi and Agya Sei had lost track of time as it was early afternoon and shadows could hardly be discerned because the sun was neither in the east nor in the west.

"You h-haven't b-been c-c-coming here lately. Why is that? Has your new p-position suddenly t-taken you away from your friends?" Akwasi asked.

"Not true, not true at all. Were it so I wouldn't be here again. In any case, it is only a week ago since you saw me here and that was because I travelled to Accra for the inauguration."

"Oh yes, I-I-I remember. How did it g-go anyway?"

"Very well indeed. It was dignifying to sit in Parliament House as the village's representative."

"How about a p-pot of palmwine? I-I don't s-suppose you feel too b-big already to drink with all your friends who were in-instrumental in g-getting you elected."

"Quite the contrary Akwasi."

Akwasi motioned to the barmaid who brought a potful instantly and a calabash for Agya Sei. Akwasi filled the calabash for Agya Sei. He took a long swig of the sweet sour foamy liquid; he controlled a belch and nodded a few times in appreciation of the quality of the wine. After the third calabash, Agya Sei felt tinkling in his mind and the environment seemed revolving and chasing invisible objects, he took a good look at Akwasi. Akwasi was the chief's son. An only son, he had been pampered from early youth and traits of that pampering which bordered on arrogance and stubbornness were still evident. For one thing, he always expected the village folk, whoever they may be, older or younger, to be the first to greet him. If they didn't, he insulted them by rolling his eyes. Akwasi possessed some diligent pride; which consciously made him maintain some distance. He was both talkative and an intent listener. His capacity for drink, especially palmwine and akpeteshie, was limitless. Although, whereas some other people become garrulous on trifles of life, he was, on the other hand, quiet under the Bacchic influence. It seemed drink could make him think better.

"Akwasi, I am going to build a house in Kumasi as quickly as I get there," he said and blew on the froth of his calabash as a tiny insect just landed in the frothy whiteness. A little wine was spilled in the process.

"Yes, I-I think you can d-do it now that you are a member of parliament, you'll have m-money and m-many contacts to b-boot."

"I am also getting tired of Abena and her children," Agya Sei said and took another quaff. "Now that I am in power I must marry again."

"W-what! D-Did I hear you right? W-what did you say again?"

"I said I must marry again."

"Ha, ha, ha, haa, haa, haa!" Akwasi laughed and then cleared his throat to get a gobful of spit. "Tsuen," he said at the same time making a loud spit. "Kai, b-but you and Abena have m-married a long time. Are you g-g-going to l-leave her or you are going to h-have two wives?"

"You speak as if the idea of two wives is an abomination for me. Doesn't your father have three wives?"

"Yes, b-but he is the chief."

"I am also a member of parliament. We wield more power than the chief and note that we are going to make legislation for you and your father, the chief, as well."

Agya Sei had a throb in the heart for his friend's apparent derision. He sat motionless as the sudden throbbing subsided. He was a man of little courage so ridicule of this sort certainly had the better of him. Now he feared to continue with Akwasi.

"Wh-who do you have in m-mind? Your wife, Abena, is j-just good enough for you. She is n-nice, beautiful and buxom and every one

4

commends her that i-i-it was your ability to look after her th-that has given her such nice qualities. What woman in the village is b-better than Abena?"

"I am not talking about a woman. I am talking about a very beautiful and educated girl. You know Abena didn't receive any formal education."

"Yiee, a g-girl?" Akwasi said and slapped his thighs loud in a banter. The same feeling of sudden fear and a throb both descended on Agya Sei again but he managed a disaffected smile.

"What is wrong with a girl?"

"I th-think Abena is j-just fine. If I had a p-person like Abena a-as a wife, nothing would deceive me to t-turn against her. Be s-satisfied with her you lusty devil. Asem beba d-dabi. (Trouble lurks) and it can s-sneak up on anyone."

"Well I am not going to leave Abena but, surely, I need a glamorous girl to join me there."

"L-L-Let me guess who this g-girl is . . . ."

"There is no need to guess, I will tell you. She is Papa Adjei's daughter whom the children call Sister Boatemaa."

There and then, Akwasi burst out into song singing:

The rain is preceeded by thunderclaps
I told you and you didn't listen
The rain is preceed by a windstorm
I told you and didn't take . . . .
I always told you and you didn't take it . . . .'

Agya Sei understood the implication of that song but he wasn't deterred. At least, that was what he felt.

"Oh c-come on, Sister Boatemaa as you c-call her is not even twenty. She has just fi-finished St. Louis Secondary School in K-Kumasi and I know . . ."

"I think she is not going to continue." Agya Sei said, not letting Akwasi finish his statements.

"I th-think she is too young and as young as sh-she is she can t-tax your energy and fi-finances. I believe you should rather co-consider sealing your t-traditional marriage with Abena in church. That way you won't think about m-marrying again because Paul, in the b-bible said if you cannot b-be like him and you have a b-burning passion, it was good to m-marry one wife."

"Where in the Bible does Paul say this?"

"In one of h-his letters."

"To which of his followers? Ephesians, Galatians, Romans or Corinthians?"

"That m-much I don't know but I've h-heard it in church often enough th-that he said it."

"You are not a good Christian then, Even I who don't go to church am better."

"If you were b-better you wouldn't th-think of d-disappointing a good wife like Abena."

"How would you like to be a "betweener" for me?" Agya Sei asked still intent on his strong desire of love or lust for Sister Boatemaa.

"No, I can't b-be a match maker for you. What happened to your c-courage?"

Courage, yes he heard it. It was an elusive quality especially when it came to this matter of Boatemaa. But drink always gave him a sense of euphoria and improved his confidence so as tipsy as he was he told his friend that he was going to Papa Adjei's house by all means.

"Don't go there r-right from here or he might th-think you are a b-big drunk Yei, Agya Sei, t-trouble will come someday O—O!"

"Get away with your clichés. What trouble will come?"

"Me g-get away, well, don't say I never s-said it."

"Oh get away."

"Take your t-time perhaps Boatemaa wouldn't w-want to marry you. She is too young and I can say that again."

"Don't you know reputation and money will count this time? Marry or no marry, there I am going."

"Okay, g-go, Akwasi said and burst out into song, with Bob Cole's rendition of the lizard which fell from high up on the Odum tree and asked the earth if she, the earth, was dizzy . . . ."

"You too you are something too much." Agya Sei said.

"Me, I am s-something, you'll s-see."

They both got up, said bye, while Agya Sei took the tab. The other customers were red-eyed from the drink and bantering their noisy talk away. One stood up and bogeyed to the synchronized clapping of the others. Akwasi looked back and called Agya Sei by patting his shoulders several times to have a look.

"Look at th-that beast."

"As for you everyone is an animal. Next time, you know, you'll be calling me an animal too!"

'Never, never, how c-can I call a member of parliament an animal you'll have me l-locked up."

"You better believe it, you'll be goaled if you tried."

"Shiee, shiee, shiee, as f-for you Agya Sei, I know you c-can do it to your own friend too."

Both walked about two hundred metres from the bar turned right as they came upon the footpath which branched to Papa Adjei's house. The sweaty furrowed brow of Agya Sei was being lapped by a cool breeze. Part of his cloth was fluttering in the wind. The sun was quite far gone in the west and shadows were a bit long and directed towards the east. One dilapidated and abandoned house of red clay stood in the bush. Agya Sei did not debate in his mind whether to go there. He stepped right behind one wall and hurriedly urinated. His inebriated mind had delayed his fingers in the search for his secret organ and he had urinated a bit in his boxer pants and shorts. There was an urgency in reenacting this ritual. He felt relieved of this urge and forgot to zip himself up. He made a loud noise of spit collection and purposely spat into the middle of the urine on the ground. He did this always because when he was younger, the older friends had told him that if he didn't do that a burning sensation would be created in his belly button. He knew it was pure superstition, however, it had become ritualistic just as the making of urine was for everybody. He bade farewell to Akwasi and proceeded.

CHAPTER 2

The women were pounding fufu (the staple of Ghanaians which is even eaten with soup) when Agya Sei got to Papa Adjei's house.

"Greetings to everybody."

"We respond to your greetings. What brings you here at this time?" The women pounding the fufu stopped and asked.

"Nothing is the trouble. I am just looking for Papa Adjei."

"You are very lucky, he just returned from Kumasi," the woman sitting by the mortar said.

"Where is he?"

"I will get him for you or is it a "two-man" business?"

"Yes it is. By the way is Boatemaa home?"

"She is seeing off a friend, she'll be right back. What do you want from her anyway?"

"None of your business."

"Ei, none of my business indeed," she smiled and winked as if she quite knew why the new member of parliament was at their house.

Knock, knock.

"Yes who is it? Come in."

"It's your new member of parliament."

"Oh welcome, welcome, feel at home in these humble surroundings!" Papa Adjei dropped both crutches and gingerly hopped to a stool closer to where he had offered Agya Sei a seat.

Papa Adjei had seen action before on the military expeditions for his colonial master during the Second World War. With an amputated right leg, he had found a different and rather tough world which was oblivious of the human long struggle. Since the colonial master hadn't kept his promise to the veterans on their return, he was for a short time reduced to the status of a pauper. With children and a wife to take care of, he had turned his attention from farming to the goldsmith's craft and also the weaving of kente. He was grave, silver haired and of average height. His wrinkled face and the deep gulleys of time on both cheeks and a grey moustache gave a rather deceptive view of his actual age.

"A glass of water?"

"I am not thirsty, anyway, but since you offer it I will take it. Thank you!"

"We, in this house, are faring quite okay. As our elders say, it is the visitor who gives the first "amanee" (message of a visitor to the visited).

"Yes our elders were wise indeed. There is nothing much the matter. As you know already I am the member of parliament. for Kodie and I am going to Accra to stay. As you also know my wife Abena is not educated. On account of that I have come to seek the hand of your daughter in marriage." There were butterflies in his stomach as he blurted out the words. There was a charged silence as Papa Adjei was lost in thought for wee bit. This hiatus heightened the rate at which Agya Sei's heart was beating.

"Your request is well taken however from your breadth, it is quite obvious that you've had some to drink. Are you sure that you are doing the right thing and that you actually want to marry my young Boatemaa? Why don't you go home, sleep off the booze and maybe discuss it with Abena and see what she says about it. I will wait for you tomorrow night or any time you think you are ready to come here again. Boatemaa is out by the way but as soon as she comes back I will have a word with her and I will tell you what went on then. In the meantime too, I will also consult with my wife."

Agya Sei protested to wait till Boatemaa came home but Papa Adjei urged him to go home. He reluctantly, shook the hand of Papa Adjei and stumbled on the stool on his left. Papa Adjei also stood and carefully steadied himself with Agya Sei's help and hopped to take his crutches. These wooden crutches were of immense help for him now he was greatly hoping that the member of parliament will also provide a human crutch for him. He was not going to give up his daughter that easily as perhaps, Agya Sei might think.

Papa Adjei looked in the east and saw dark and cottony clouds. He had wanted to call Agya Sei back in order not to be beaten by the impending rain but he stopped. Agya Sei had gone a while and it started to rain. At first it was a mere drizzle so he didn't think he should take cover from it. He quickened his steps and gathered the mass of his cloth closer to himself. It didn't stop raining. It had even intensified. Agya Sei was slowly getting wet and as far he had gone there wasn't any cover in sight. Whichever way he went, backwards or forwards, he knew he was going to be drenched. He walked home.

When Agya Sei got home, for no reason, he yelled at Abena:

"Won't you bring me a towel? You silly and daft woman. Take my cloth, swine." He said to his wife on arrival.

"Don't call me silly, daft or swine. It is the same "swine" lady who has made you what you are today."

"What have you done for me? Your soup has never been palatable anyway since I married you even though I give you enough "chop money" for the market."

"Ei, as for today I don't know how to cook according to you. I thank you very much. I thank you."

"You thank whom? Foolish woman. Take the cloth." Agya Sei threw the cloth at Abena. She ducked to the left and the cloth fell in the mud. Agya Sei was angry and had wanted to deal Abena a blow but for the timely intervention of his son Kwaku who quickly collected the wet cloth from the mud.

Abena was ignorant of her husband's intentions and had quite rightly been stupefied by his apparent belligerency. He called for his food, ate it hurriedly and retired to bed.

The cool harmattan night lulled him to sleep while the birds sang their final lullabies to give way to the crickets and geckoes to continue for the night. The frogs and toads belched out their sonorous and disharmonious sounds in welcome of the recent downpour. Serene darkness shrouded living and non living things alike and offered slumber to Agya Sei and others for a sound repose. Nevertheless, Agya Sei's sleep was not all that sound because he became restless and dreamed negatively about his proposed marriage with Boatemaa.

He dreamt that he was quite young—about the same age as Boatemaa. There had been a traditional dance and all was going well. He had, all the time, danced with other girls and finally he was going to try his luck with Boatemma. Immediately he went closer to her, the big black bull belonging to Auntie Ama whom everybody at Kodie labeled as a witch, came out of nowhere charging at him. All the other boys and girls got out of its way but it was still charging and gaining on Agya Sei. Unfortunately for Agya Sei, he was wearing a red outfit, and couldn't run fast enough but he managed to get to the fence of Yaw Panin, Papa Adjei's friend's farm. There and then, the bull was close enough to deal him a butt in the butt. Just at this point, he was awakened by the noise of Abena who was also preparing to get to bed. He was quite shaken and blessed himself for waking up. The first thing he thought were the witches and other evil spirits. He had never been on good terms with Auntie Ama just because she was suspect as a witch. He concluded that she wished him evil and thus the morbid encounter with her bull in the nightmare. How realistic it appeared in the dream and how uncharacteristic it actually is in real life. He lay awake now and debated in his mind as to whether it was too hasty to tell Abena of what he had been planning all along. He mustered enough courage and said,

"Abena, I am going to Accra and I want you to stay here with the children."

"Why is that? But I can be of good help to you there while you go on your business as an M.P."

"Yes, as an MP I am a sophisticated person and Accra is also sophisticated. Actually, what I want to tell you is that I need a sophisticated partner to go with this place and new reputation."

"Let me guess, you are thinking of marrying another wife more educated and more sophisticated as you call it." A dead silence ensued but Agya Sei broke it and said,

"You guessed right. I intend to seek the hand of Boatemaa, Papa Adjei's daughter. I have gone to her father and I am going there again. I just had to discuss it with you." The impact of this disclosure was too hard to bear. Agya Sei surely, callously, and brusquely knew how to bring pain to a person even if it was his wife of twenty five years. Things were not going to be the same, of course. He was aware of them but he didn't care. He knew definitely that two of his children were older than Boatemaa but he did not care as well. Abena had been quiet all this time but She calmly began to speak even though she was hurt and disappointed.

"What makes you think that she'll go for this?"

"Money talks, reputation talks. I am an important person now, remember." He said it callously with eyes wide open quite oblivious of his wife's anguish.

"Now I understand why you said my soup wasn't palatable despite the fact you've eaten it for twenty five years and over. If fairness is the question, then you are not being fair to me at all. I warn you to be very careful with your recent attitude and decisions because I think this member of parliament business has gone into your head. What will your children think about you? What will others, your own peers, think about you?"

"It is not a question of what other people think about me. It is a practical question of what partner can best take up the job of a member of parliament's wife in a fashionable and glamorous way. Boatemaa is the only one in this area who fits all these descriptions."

"Polygamy or bigamy abound in the land but let me tell you, there are problems and dangers that are concomitant with the polygamous and the people around him. If I had my own way, I would say let this decision get out of your mind once and for all. But if you still insist I will give you the go-ahead. Afterall I am always the senior wife. I have control of the household."

She said and turned towards the wall away from her husband to sleep and sobbing in the process.

"My mind is made up. I will do what I please," he said and drew his cloth over his head.

"Well, it's up to you."

The next morning Agya Sei was still determined to have his way. Akwasi, dressed in his old blue sweater, caught up with him on the way to Papa Adjei's house.

"G-Good m-morning chum."

Agya Sei nodded in greeting. "And how are you this brisk morning?"

"F-fine. What happened with Papa Adjei and Boatemaa?"

Agya Sei shrugged. "Boatemaa wasn't home. I suppose it's just was well, since I wasn't very sober. Papa Adjei advised me to come back. He didn't tell me no so that give me hope."

"Didn't I t-tell you not t-to go there yesterday?" Akwasi gestured and said.

"I've gone over one hurdle already because I have discussed it with Abena. I told her last night. I made her cry."

"And y-y-you weren't b-bothered by it. What was her r-reaction?"

"Naturally, she would feel bad but I succeeded in winning her consent."

"I f-feel bad for h-her too. I still think y-you are not being fair t-to her."

"Don't worry she'll get used to it."

Akwasi could see a definite strain of confidence in Agya Sei. His new role as the important person in the area had made him not to see any disappointments and grief which could come. However, he wished Agya Sei good luck again since his advice had fallen on deaf ears.

Agya Sei had seen Boatemaa many times. Her beauty and polite personality befuddled him. The children called her Sister Boatemaa out of respect. She was a tall girl. With slim long legs, she also had a very generous helping of buttocks. What gave Agya Sei a stirring in the loins was the way they shook at her every calculated step. Her bigger—than—average breasts were pointed and curved upwards. Her arms came down her slim chest with grace. Her pleasant face displayed black eyes with pearly whiteness, her teeth and gums wee in direct contrast of white and black and she always had a beautiful coiffeured hair on her magnificent head that was propped up by a long neck. Her command of the native language and English taking into consideration that she was only a high school graduate was impeccable. She was both polite and courteous. However, these attributes were not signs of a weak personality thus she appealed to everyone.

Agya Sei was still sitting in front of the mirror in his room ruminating. In his hand was an old picture. He was then like a mannequin with women not a trifle problematic to him. Although the picture had a crease in it, it showed him as the ultimate in handsomeness. He had a dark and flush glossy hair carefully coiffeured to the then latest style. He himself had told his children that the style was the "Tokyo Joe". He had cut in the middle of that flush top hair a straight route which, thanks to some sharp scissors, found its way not quite to the back of the head but close enough. He had thick eye brows which even today he moves up and down in quick succession to coerce a protracted stare and a smile from the little ones. To the young women, this ploy was a different story because that alone had brought him many a strong romance with them. He remembered them all. His huge shoulders and square and deep chest needed only that kind of thick neck which supported the cradle of his intellect. He wore a white half unbuttoned shirt to expose his hairy chest and a copper necklace. His whole stature from the chest down to the pelvis was an isosceles triangle with the base up. He had a bit bandy legs all of which were good attractions for a man in his village.

Now, though, his flush hair was only apparent on the sides and back only for, at sixty, a bald pate added a distinguished trait to his features despite the main idea that, to him, it was a calamity. For what will Boatemaa say about this condition akin to old age. Regardless of the fact that he always applied "yoomo" (the local black dye), streaks of grayish hair strands could still be found. 'Is it a plus or a minus when my heart yearns For a girl with standing breasts and well endowed rear end.' But as he sat brooding over old age traits, he managed a smile and in the mirror, he still discovered and found hope in his soft but pronounced dimples on both cheeks, and his front gap teeth which his cheered him up a great deal. His shoulders were still square, the hair on the hands and chest hadn't disappeared. The legs were still bandy and, oh yes, the very deep voice. A new surge of confidence galore started to rise in him so win or no win, Boatemaa or bust!

His anxiety to see Papa Adjei and Boatemaa was revealed in his frantic preparations that day. He took a bath and ironed one of his best trousers and shirts. He did his manicure and pedicure and polished his shoes. He put perfume in his handkerchief, and also powdered his armpits with fragrant talcum powder. Agya Sei was really in love. Although contrary to popular belief, a man his age could fall desperately in love as he was displaying. Love knows no age, he thought.

When evening came, he went through his dinner rapidly and said goodbye to Abena who had been stupefied by her husband's doings. He walked with new confidence, whistling the local rendition of "Que sera, sera" to Papa Adjei's house. Papa Adjei hadn't finished his day's weaving. He still went thus with his loom,

> Kro, kro, kro, kro, hi hi hi hi
> Krohin krohin ko ko kro hi hi
> Krohin ko . . . .

He threw the shuttle from left to right and was slowly getting perpendicular patterns in the red and blue yarn. He was unaware that Agya Sei had greeted him with a warm good evening so Agya Sei had to repeat it. This time he heard it and stopped weaving.

"Hello, hello, good evening," he said and picked up his crutches and labored out of the loom.

"You look nice this evening," he said to Agya Sei.

"Thank you."

"Let's go in, should we."

When seated, Papa Adjei disclosed to Agya Sei what he and his wife had discussed during the day but Agya Sei insisted that Papa Adjei call his wife and Boatemaa. Just as Agya Sei finished saying this, Papa Adjei's wife got in followed by Boatemaa as if there had been some telepathic communication between them and Agya Sei. Boatemaa was looking her best.

"As you know already, Agya Sei was here last night and we discussed things about what he said but could we hear it from his own mouth again. Agya Sei you can set the ball rolling."

"Thank you for your warm hospitality. It is most pleasant for me to be back in your presence again. As I told you previously, this concerns myself, my new position and your daughter. I have watched her a lot since the elections. Considering her education, her own prettiness and the singular way she comports herself, I have thought about her her again and again. On account of these facts I can't go on circumnavigating on the issues any longer. Our wisest elders were generally brief so I will cut it short by saying I came to ask the hand of your daughter in marriage."

Boatemaa was flattered and tickled by yet Agya Sei's attention and persistence.

"Well, Boatemaa, as a linquist who doesn't know how to talk, it's all in your ears," Papa Adjei said.

"I beg you Dada, thanks. I am excited about the prospects of marriage right after school. Considering the current economic stringencies in the country the young men are hesitant and unadventurous to come forward and take up responsibility. However, I am young and I know I am beautiful because many people in Kumasi and here tell me. Agya Sei is a hardworking man. He is also married with children some of whom are older than myself.' Agya Sei felt a lump in his throat and cleared it. A heat wave traveled his whole body and sweat instantly formed on his hands and brows.

"He is an experienced man which is much to his credit. His age, however, makes me think twice," Agya Sei dropped his gaze to the floor and felt a rapidly beating heart.

"What are my friends and school mates going to say when they hear of our being together? Definitely, they will say I've married not for love but rather for money and thus I am a gold digger. I would like to have some time for myself to think things over with some of my friends, and I hope to give you an answer at a later date. Dada, I beg you, this is what I have to say."

"Agya Sei, you heard what she said. Girls of this age want to make decisions on their own and, rightly, we can't prevent them from doing so. We can only give them counseling and little guidance. It's their life. Their generation is different from ours. We have got to a point where we display a taedium vitae sometimes but they are only beginning." Agya Sei lifted up his head and deliberately avoided Boatemaa's gaze and said,

"Your daughter has spoken as a mature lady. Her words only give me hope and not discouragement. I still look forward to a positive answer because it would be to her benefit and yours to have me in your family circles. Money will not be a problem and I intend to build a house for her if she accepts." Agya Sei said this, though, his usual liveliness seemed missing. He was resolved to have a young wife like Boatemaa. He was well aware of the talks about "sugar daddies". In fact, he used to condemn these elderly men who relished on the fact that young girls could yield to their whims and caprices. Now, though, he was confronted with the idea of becoming one. It doesn't matter, he thought, it is only one of the facts of life which creep up suddenly on older men of success. He went home quite uncertain about himself. At home, he feigned annoyance at Abena who asked.

"How was your self imposed mission?" Abena said and feigned a smile.

"It's none of your business."

"It is surely my business to know, you're my husband and matters that concern you also concern me. Were you successful or were you not? Ha ha."

"Don't embarrass me in front of the children." At bedtime he told Abena all that had transpired between him and Papa Adjei's household. At the realization of a possible negative answer from Boatemaa she thought she could revive the interest in each other which was almost tapering into nothingness. What she thought made sense but it could also lack conviction.

CHAPTER 3

Agya Sei's cocoa farms were luxuriant and bustling with vivacity. The cocoa farms brought him most of his money and he was wealthy because cocoa, being the cash crop in Ghana always brought him a lot. Instead of being stereotypic in his work he also had a poultry, a piggery and a large fish pond for breeding and cultivating some varieties of tilapia and cat fish.

This morning his hired hands were unusually late so he decided to do some cleaning rounds himself. Previously, he had asthmatic bouts but he couldn't figure out how and why they happened.

First, with the help of his son, Kwaku, he picked up the eggs from the layers. They were doing a magnificent job because some had laid two or three eggs and Agya Sei and his son were particularly happy about it. Agya Sei attributed this to his hardy stock of chicken, the good feed he gave them, the clean supply of water and all his veterinary attention.

"Carefully take this container of eggs inside and bring a new basket." He said to Kwaku. He gingerly lifted the basket on to his son's head, and advised him once again to be careful.

"Bring the brooms too, will you?"

Kwaku took the eggs to the room and returned with brooms and a dust collector. Agya Sei took hold of one broom, shooed the chickens away, and made space to clean. He had cleaned for a short while and he started to have difficulty in breathing. The condition intensified. The nearness of his asthma was close. He sat down heavily on a stump and wheezed and wheezed.

"What is it dada?" Kwaku asked.

"Bring me my inhaler," he said with considerable difficulty. Fortunately, Abena was coming by and helped him on his feet and meticulously got him into his room. After a few deep oral inhalations, his condition was almost better but not quite so. As distressing as asthma is Agya Sei felt weak. He had to have a trip to the hospital. Abena, a loving wife and as sympathetic as she was, quickly sent Kwaku to get the driver of the only taxi in the village. She helped Agya Sei to get in his travel-worth attire and off they went as soon as the taxi driver arrived. They headed towards Kumasi with Okomfo Anokye Hospital as their destination.

On arrival, Agya Sei seemed better however, the doctor gave him shots of aminophylline and also some Ventolin and Franol tablets. He was on admission for one night and Abena stayed with him all through the night with herself not getting a wink of sleep. One might think her loving attitude and concern would sway Agya Sei from his marital quests for Boatemaa but no he was not bothered about this. Despite the fact that his condition was chronic, he attributed this bout to the witch Auntie Ama, who he always blamed for every misfortune he encountered. More important to Agya Sei was not the asthma but the need for the love of Boatemaa and thank God his asthma was only a spell. But that spell seemed to him ages and couldn't wait to be back to Kodie and thoughts about Boatemaa were his standard hope. When they were on the way home he asked Abena:

"Have you seen Boatemaa lately?"

"Don't worry me with Boatemaa you have a one track mind. Boatemaa today, Boatemaa yesterday, and Boatemaa tomorrow. I am tired of it all. Don't you even think about your condition and my help which I have patiently and diligently given you over the years. You think you are doing a good thing. You will see."

"I won't see anything. I am decided and I can't go back on my decision."

"Let's get home, there is no need for a marital tiff right in the taxi. It is not good for the driver to see our dirty linen so beat it."

Agya Sei was quiet and soon he was dozing. It later developed into a loud stertorous snore. The driver turned his head back once in a while to see Agya Sei. Abena let him snore on. A little dream was being screened in Agya Sei's sleep and he was smiling like a baby does. Abena nudged him in the side and asked why he was smiling. He told of the dream and another encounter with Boatemaa.

"Ei, Boatemaa again," she said, "you will crack up with thoughts about her. Don't say I never said it." His smile was another malignant one. They got home in one piece.

It is three weeks after Agya Sei went to see Papa Adjei for the second time. Nothing had come from Boatemaa and, as usual, he had many thoughts about her. The outcome of his cogitations was that he would seek a quiet drink with his friend Akwasi. It was both warm and humid and palm wine would taste very good moreover, the seller had relayed to Agya Sei the message of a fresh tap.

He put on his cloth and went to look for his drinking partner whom he met shortly after leaving home.

"How is it today? How about a couple of calabashfuls at Owuo's bar? He has a new tap," he said.

"Sh-sure I can go for a c-c-calabashful or two. I-I-It's a hot a-afternoon," he said. The bar was full and vibrant. There were the reserved seats. So the two friends went and sat there. The barmaid brought a potful and two calabashes. Agya Sei tipped her after she said, 'enjoy yourselves.'

"It's thoughts about Boatemaa that bring me here. She is unduly tardy with an answer."

"Ei, B-Boatemaa will k-kill you. Take your time. She'll c-come to it. Our elders used t-to say that if a woman k-keeps long in th-the bathroom it is b-because she is m-making her toilet. She knows the reason for th-the delay so exercise a little p-patience."

"Should I wait till she comes to me or I can go to her. For as the saying goes "if the mountains won't go to Mohammed, Mohammed will go to the mountains.""

'You c-can wait a we-we-week more, if she hasn't c-c-come forth then you c-can go to her." To turn around the conversation Akwasi said, "By th-the way how is your p-proposed house in Kumasi going to b-be like?"

"It is going to be a storey building and a nice one too. Your father is helping me to arrange a plot of land at exclusive Asokwa near the Kumasi Sports Stadium, if he hasn't told you already."

"Oh I-I-I didn't know this b-before. Asokwa is a very nice p-place, There are some magnificent b-buildings around the stadium. I've b-been there several times."

"Building a house is a tough decision. Cement costs are exorbitant let alone labor and lumber," Agya Sei said.

"I hear it c-costs over fifty million c-cedis to build a b-boys quarters. A story b-building will b-be in the n—neighborhood of one hundred million and fifty cedis, where are you g-going to g-get all that money?"

"The farms will be partly responsible. But why do you ask? I am a member of parliament and money will surely come through contacts and gifts after I've done favors for people."

"It is th-th-the order of the d-d-day, isn't it?"

"Yes what else? It is our turn now," Agya Sei said with a wide smile and seemed to enjoy the fact that he had won an opportunity for self-aggrandizement. Meanwhile, the barmaid brought another potful but Agya Sei gestured that they still had a bit of the last pot left. She took it back.

Just there two relatively drunk guys who had been arguing about the elections and why Agya Sei shouldn't have won the were fighting. One who used to date Boatemaa and appeared not to like Agya Sei said,

"I know what he is going to do at parliament house in Accra. He is going to steal all the money and he is an "awengaa" (child molester).

"Why do you say that about Agya Sei?"

They kept arguing. It became a fist fight.

The taller man got hold of the shorts of his friend and roughed him up squarely. The shorter man headed his friend in the chin and he bit his tongue so he dealt the shorter one a sharp box to the ear. Recoiling from the pain, he went for his friends legs and by some weird act, they were both on the ground. Akwasi, who had been studying both men got up and rushed to them. With one heave he got both up and threw them against the outside wall of the bar. The two men struggled to get out of the strong hold of Akwasi but his strength proved decisive.

"Get out of th-th b-bar," he said. Akwasi took both of them outside the bar, released his hold on the taller man and urged him to stay away from the bar and away from his so-called friend. Akwasi got back to his seat and all the men clapped at his effort to keep peace. He raised his hand in acknowledgement of the applause.

When he sat down he still wanted to take Agya Sei off the thoughts of Boatemaa so he asked:

"Why, y-your eldest son h-h-has kept s-so long abroad. Hasn't he finished hi-his education?"

"If the foreigner does not go back to his home, he is despised and called a slave, He'll come someday I am sure."

"What is h-he s-studying again?"

25

'When he left home his intentions were set on becoming a medical doctor. The last time he wrote, he said he had finished two degrees in Biology and Classics."

"Too much education is b-b-bad. Children should l-learn traditional norms and not white man's c-civilization."

"Yes, I didn't go abroad or anything but look at me now. I am better than most of them. However, what makes people laugh somewhere makes people weep somewhere too. Going to the white man's land will make many people laugh and people will loathe just staying behind in the village but we enjoy it. Anyway, let's call it quits after this calabash."

"Fine wi-with me."

Agya Sei took the tab again and out they went.

The week that intervened came quickly almost catching Agya Sei by surprise. He carefully dressed to purposely impress Boatemaa again. When he walked to Papa Adjei's house, he coincidentally met Boatemaa on the way and asked: "What possible excuse have you for keeping so long with an answer?" Agya Sei said with some confidence.

"I beg you, none, except my mind has been distraught with happenings in my family, and I felt utterly incapable of giving you the attention that you deserved to expect from me," she said apologetically.

"Is this the reason why I have not seen you?"

"I beg you, not quite, I consulted with my friends too and I was so pre-occupied that I feared if I came to you my decision would be precipitous." For a moment Agya Sei was silent then he asked slowly: "Does that mean that you do not wish to be my lover and wife?" he asked calmly while he became conscious of her dark loveliness.

"I beg you, my parents will have the last say but let's go to them. I'll tell you my part of it." Agya Sei sighed and flattered her by saying,

"I have never concealed my appreciation for you from you and you always arouse in me a greater degree of affection than I have ever known before." Boatemaa, obviously flattered, smiled and thanked him. Agya Sei was a bit relieved because he saw a positive sign woven in that smile.

'Let's go, and I'll follow you," he said. When they got home, Papa Adjei was reclining on a lazy chair. He picked up his crutches immediately when he saw Agya Sei with his daughter.

"Good evening," Agya Sei said.

"Good evening. Boatemaa call your mother and bring a chair for Agya Sei."

"I beg you, OK."

"One must prepare before taking up an arduous task. One never says to a person to go away with his goodness. Boatemaa has said yes but that's not it because we the parents have our conditions. The conditions I am afraid, are tough ones," Papa Adjei hopped on his left leg to his sideboard. There he produced a long white sheet with a list and gave it to Agya Sei. The positive answer from Boatemaa made Agya Sei beam with a smile. He carefully read the list nodding once and again. A house for Boatemaa was one condition but he had promised that once already. A car and a trip abroad were also included in the list. A separate bank account for Boatemaa and regular monetary gifts to her parents.

Agya Sei sat quietly for a while digesting the message of the list. Papa Adjei and wife nodded as he picked up his crutches to go out for a moment to ease himself.

"Do you agree or you don't" Boatemaa's mother asked.

"Did you plan this with your husband?"

"Yes."

"It's quite demanding."

"I know but we've worked very hard for Boatemaa."

"I know she is worth a lot but not this much."

Papa Adjei entered, placed his crutches against the wall and hopped once again to his seat.

"Well Agya Sei, do you agree?"

"Well but—,"

"But what?"

"I've come a long way but, as for this, I don't think I will go for them."

"Please I didn't hear you," Papa Adjei said.

"Did you say no?" the wife contributed.

"Yes, I did."

"Oh please, why?" asked the wife.

"I love your daughter but not that much considering all these conditions."

"Oh please, we are prepared to compromise."

"No, I think I must be going."

"Oh please, Agya Sei, please," Boatemaa's mother said.

"I beg you, Agya Sei listen to my parents."

"No." After Agya Sei had said this he got up suddenly and made for the doorway.

"Please, we beg you," Boatemaa and her mother said together.

"No. Somebody might do all these for her but not me, after all I promised to build her a house and if that's not enough then I can't be enslaved by your conditions." Agya Sei opened the door and said, "I am sorry." He stepped outside and a good and cool breeze welcomed him.

"I beg you dada, it is your list that has brought about this stalemate. I beg you, my friends know that I am lucky to be thrust into money and fame but now as it looks, he has backed off. It will be very hard to explain this to them. Couldn't you send him a delegation to try and get him to rescind his decision and save the situation."

"You are quite clever for your good thinking because I was thinking on the same lines. We must go to Agya Sei," Papa Adjei said, a bit confused.

Was Agya Sei's attitude a bluff or he actually meant it. It is obvious that Agya Sei has to let Abena know about it but he only told her a lie.

Papa Adjei and wife, a bit embarrassed, decided on Boatemaa's proposal. They thought it inappropriate to go to Agya Sei themselves, as by now, they were unsure of unpredictable Agya Sei who seemed to be much in love. They started to plan. Papa Adjei's wife brought an idea.

"Why don't we seek the help of Boatemaa's uncle and wife to send a 'dwantoa" (urging a person to rescind a decision) for us and on behalf of his niece."

"Yes I think that will do because I know Agya Sei thinks well of him. In fact he campaigned for him during the elections."

Papa Adjei got on his crutches and slowly walked towards his brother's house. His wife followed. At Boatemaa's uncle's house Papa Adjei sadly narrated the missed chance of this eligible Agya Sei.

"Don't worry that much. I think I can help. But why didn't you tell me of the marriage proposal anyway before this time?"

CHAPTER 4

Soon, Agya Sei will be leaving for Accra and as the village's soccer manager, the two teams in the village decided to play a farewell match for him as an honor to celebrate his victory at the elections and before he left for Accra, the capital. The coach of Shooting Stars, Agya Sei's own team, formally came to Agya Sei's house to invite him.

"In a couple of weeks' time, we want to put up a good show so we have intensified training and the boys are really geared up towards this," the coach said.

"Don't you think we should have new jerseys for the players?" Agya Sei asked noticing that, previously, Their old jerseys weren't good for the event.

"We can borrow some jerseys from Kotoko Babies in Kumasi," the coach said.

"No, we can't kowtow to what they say since you know by, all means, they will come up with unnecessary conditions. They will be asking for money. We must get our own jerseys," Agya Sei said.

"How?"

"Remember, I bought the old ones for them."

"Oh yes, I remember quite well."

"What makes you think I can't do it again?"

"Really! If you mean it then I can go to Kumasi to buy them."

"I will go with you because I know you might buy cheap ones and pocket the rest of the money."

The coach couldn't wait to bring the news to his team. In the evening, he gathered them together and broke the news. To their surprise, Agya Sei also got to the playing field to watch the team to see if the boys were good enough so that buying the jerseys would be worth it. The boys really played hard. Agya Sei promised them that other than the jerseys, he would give every player a monetary gift if they won.

After the day's training session, Agya Sei called the coach and the captain to accompany him the next day to make the purchases. On, Monday, the three were off to Kumasi. They combed store after store to get their items. They came to a store with black and white jerseys but Agya Sei almost declined to buy them because they looked too much like the jerseys of Kumasi Cornerstones.

"We need to look like Kotoko. It is my team and I know with red outfits they will play just like Kotoko."

"Why do you say that, because my boys never go to watch Kotoko in Kumasi! I think any number of new jerseys will do.' The coach was able to coerce Agya Sei to agree to that so they bought fifteen black and white tops and blue shorts with white trimmings. It was a top secret for everyone in the team. They wanted to give a big surprise to the chief and his son who were patrons of the other team, "Mighty Eagles."

Eagerness and anxiety made the teams itch for the day of the match. When the day came, everyone feared that the rains would be a threat but in an hour or so the cloudy skies cleared and there was a nice breeze to ease the mugginess. Everybody agreed that it had rained elsewhere and that the gods had spared the occasion.

After Agya Sei saw his team train, he was sure of victory, so he got the chief and Akwasi into a gamble. He betted ten million cedis each with the chief and Akwasi so the match added a new importance for them.

Almost the whole village gathered to watch the match. The chief's linguist poured libation to the gods and ancestors to rid the match of injuries and other unwanted events.

Mighty Eagles were the first to get on the field wearing all green jerseys and black shorts. The delay to come on the field by Shooting Stars made angers rise. Akwasi was particularly angry but he was cooled down by his father and other supporters of Mighty Eagles. The referee blew his whistle again and again. Finally, Shooting Stars emerged wearing their new strip. A little commotion ensued. There was a lineup of the teams and someone who was lucky to have a camera took pictures. After inspection of the teams by the chief, Agya Sei was made to take the kick off. Everything was perfect and the game got underway.

Shooting Stars kicked off first and the players passed the ball from the centre circle all the way to the goalkeeper. There were whistles and catcalls from the spectators. The goalkeeper bounced the ball a few times and punted a hard high ball. The inside right dummied to the left and stylishly dribbled past the opponent. He kicked a long ball to his wing who raced past two defenders and laid a pass to his centre forward. He took the pass on the volley and sent a thunderbolt towards goal. The goalkeeper, almost off his mark dived to the right and collected the shot as cooly as a cat. Shooting Stars were incensed by the early onslaught and attacked furiously. But for the goalkeeper of Mighty Eagles, Eagles would have conceded three goals in fifteen minutes. The game pressed on.

A faulty pass by a midfielder caused a counter attack by the Eagles. An overlapping left back laid a perfect pass to his center half who drove a grasscutting pile driver to the left of the goalkeeper of Shooting Stars. The goalie made a dive and almost grabbed the ball but he fumbled. The ball hit the left woodwork and yes, it was in the net. 'GOAL!' One nil. Mighty Eagles.

The dejected goalkeeper collected the ball from the net and kicked it towards the center. Meanwhile the strikers of Mighty Eagles hadn't finished celebrating the goal. One cheerleader shot onto the field and hugged the goal scorer. There were cheers everywhere especially in the corner of the chief and Akwasi. It was a good beginning for them in keeping with a hopeful win at the betting.

Shooting Stars were relentless in their attacks. Their midfield was superb but their defense was a bit suspect. Mighty Eagles depended on their fast counter attacks which gave the goalie of Shooting Stars a very busy day. The sweeper for the Eagles was the backbone of his team because he could ward off most of the attacks of Shooting Stars and send the ball away for a fast attack.

A few minutes before half time, three minutes to be precise, a blunder by the left full back of Shooting Stars made the opposing inside right head home for a goal. The referee disallowed it whistling for offside. Immediately, two of the forwards of Eagles rushed towards the referee. At that excited moment one forward punched the referee in the face and he almost fell. With lightning speed, Akwasi was on the field to keep peace. In the meantime, the referee had raised his red card to the Eagles' striker and he was sent off the field. That uncalled for episode nearly marred the first half but the game got underway again without much excitement. In a short time, the referee whistled for the end of the half.

During the recess, the coach and Agya Sei gave Shooting Stars a good harangue. The coach threatened to replace anyone who didn't play up to par with the others. So there was frenzy in their camp and everybody determined to die a little for Agya Sei. The coach for Mighty Eagles was not complacent at all by the one goal lead so he came up with good strategies to offset the Shooting Stars midfield and save their sweeper form too much work. His men were gingered up even though they were left with ten men.

The referee whistled and the players jogged onto the field and took their positions. Eagles' forwards took the kick off. A pass to the left wing was intercepted by a Shooting Star defender who headed the ball to his number six. He chested the ball nicely and kicked it to his left winger. He changed the direction of attack and lobbed a high one to the right. The center forward was there and maneuvered around two defensemen. He was almost going round a third defender but the defender sacrificed a professional foul by pulling the shirt of the Shooting Stars' player. The infringement was quickly taken but it was intercepted. Eagles had the ball. They were pushing and pressing forward. The sweeper gave an overhead pass to his number six. Number six dribbled past an opponent and feinted to pass the ball to his center forward and unloaded a terrific shot. The distance and angle of the ball caught the Shooting Stars' goalie asleep. The ball sailed past the right post and into the upper corner of the net.

"Goal!" The shouts from most of the spectators was simultaneous and deafening. Agya Sei wiped his brow and furtively looked in the chief's and Akwasi's corner. They thought they had the match all wrapped up. They were shaking hands.

The coach of Shooting Stars quickly made two changes bringing on a defender and a striker. That seemed a very good decision because this striker combined effectively with his other forwards and pulled one back in only ten minutes.

There were fifteen minutes left for the end of the match and Shooting Stars were trailing by a goal. They were bombarding the goal area of Mighty Eagles with well calculated shots. Their efforts paid off and Mighty Eagles conceded three corners in a row. The third corner was taken shortishly. Almost all the players of Shooting Stars were in the half of their opponents. The inside left of Stars gave a telling pass to his inside right after dribbling past a defender. The inside right laid a magnificent grounder to the left. The shot ricocheted off the sweeper of Eagles who, as usual, was bound on another interception. The ball went straight into the net. The goalie did not have a chance as he had already dived to the right of the goal posts.

GOAL!!! Supporters of the Stars including Agya Sei rushed to the field and carried their forwards shoulder high. It took a good six minutes before the referee and linesmen and other self appointed policemen were able to quell the hub-bub. There were five minutes remaining and there was a ding dong battle on the field. Mighty Eagles had all their men in defense and rather worn out. Most of the time, they just kicked the ball into touch for a throw-in or a corner. They were able to hang on to the two-two draw. The teams were headed for the taking of penalties as it was getting too late for extra time. The referee got five players from each team, whistled for every spectator to clear off the field and placed the ball at the penalty spot in the west end of the field. First to take a shot was Shooting Stars. The player made no mistake and the ball was in the net. Three, two Shooting Stars.

The Shooting Stars took to the line and put up a little show to put fear in the player of Mighty Eagles' goalie who was next to take a shot. He took a magnificent left footer which beat the goalie. Three, Three.

The goalie for Mighty Eagles saved the next penalty so it was advantage Mighty Eagles. A shot from number 10 of Mighty Eagles increased the tally to four-three Mighty Eagles. Anxieties were running high in the camp of Shooting Stars. To take the next penalty was Number 5 for the Stars. He went to the ball, took it and placed it back again as if to say the ball wasn't on the right spot. He took four steps back. The referee whistled and he shot straight into the hands of the Eagles' goalie. But the referee awarded a new kick as he maintained that the goalie moved before the kick was taken. The Eagles' coach vehemently protested but the referee stood his ground and ordered the coach off the field. The Stars' player was nervous because much depended on him. The referee placed the ball on the spot and the Stars' player moved back crossing himself. He kicked a high ball which was punched over the crossbar by the Eagles' goalie. The Shooting Stars' player broke into tears. It was a save for Mighty Eagles but that wasn't the end of the game. They had to score on their last spotkick to win.

The chief, Akwasi and other supporters of Eagles had their fingers crossed for the coup-de-grace of Shooting Stars. Much depended on this goal for the gamblers. Everything was calm and quiet. The referee had the ball. He walked slowly to the penalty spot and carefully placed it. Eagles' number 6 was to take the kick. He went to the referee for a short time. One wondered what he told the referee. He jumped up a few times and walked towards the ball. The walk turned into a slow run and he blasted a thunderous shot. G O A L!!! G O A L!! G O A L!!! The goalie had no chance at all. There was jubilation everywhere for this triumph. The chief, Agya Sei and Akwasi shook the hands of the worn out players and Agya Sei presented the trophy to the captain of the Eagles. Agya Sei had lost the game and the bet. He just couldn't accept defeat. He was disconsolate and thought much after the match. But the football match taught Agya Sei a lot about life itself. One thing he learned was that you cannot always have situations and life the way you want them because there are bound to be disappointments and one has to brace oneself for any eventualities and regard life with earnest hope because politics in Africa can be very difficult and dangerous sometimes.

CHAPTER 5

Wofa Atta, Boatemaa's uncle, got two very respectable people in the village to accompany him to Agya Sei's house. They called on him on Tuesday evening when Abena had finished cooking the evening meal and Agya Sei was about to eat.

"Good evening Agya Sei."

"Good evening. You are invited to join me with this meal."

"We are not hungry and thanks anyway," Wofa Atta said.

"I insist because our culture deems it fit for the visitor to partake in a meal with his host."

"Okay since you insist we'll wash our hands and join in," said Wofa Atta again.

Agya Sei dished part of the fufu into his newly bought pyrex bowl, put some soup and beef and "akrantie" (grasscutter) on the visitors' food. They munched away delectably amid trivial conversation as if they had forgotten the reason why they were under Agya Sei's roof.

After they finished eating and drinking cool water from the earthenware pot, Agya Sei asked "amanee." (the word from the visitor to the visited)

"Thank you for your kind hospitality. We are on a big mission on behalf of my niece, Boatemaa and, of course Papa Adjei's household."

"Oh about the marriage proposal again, isn't it?"

"Yes," two of the visitors responded simultaneously. "Papa Adjei narrated his side of the story to us, and we thought that there was a shortcoming somewhere," Wofa Atta said.

"Yes the conditions," Agya Sei said. Just then Abena came into the room and they asked her to sit in on the discussion. Immediately she became aware of the item of discussion, she excused herself and went out again never to return until the three men left.

"Papa Adjei is ready to compromise, Agya Sei, and he certainly wants you to be in his family circles. That's why he didn't waste too much time in asking us to come with a 'dwantoa' to you," again Wofa Atta said.

"Yes, I have come a long way in this marriage business. I like and love Boatemaa and want to do a lot for her, however, if Papa Adjei insists on a foreign trip and regular monetary gifts to him and his wife, then I think he is going too far."

"We understand your point but if Papa Adjei expects money, we think it is quite understandable. Look at his condition. Don't you feel something for him," one of Wofa Atta's friends contributed.

"One shouldn't feel sorry for a person just because he has a disability. I have always admired Papa Adjei's courage. Other people would have easily done nothing and become beggars but this is not so in his case. It is quite commendable that he earns his living in dignitiy. If he will scrap the foreign trip and the money to them I will agree to his 'dwantoa,'" said Agya Sei.

"Oh, I am quite sure Papa Adjei will agree to this. If you make the bride price big enough there won't be any cause for compliant," Wofa Alta said.

"Sure, you'll have it."

"You are not such a bad bargainer afterall. In fact, we were afraid that our mission wouldn't be successful but you've proved to be kindhearted. We are proud and rather thankful to take the message to Papa Adjei, his wife and Boatemaa." Wofa Atta said. "We also invite you to bring the drinks the bride price and everything that custom demands to Boatemaa's parents."

"I will do it as soon as possible because it won't be long and I will be away in Accra and surely with her."

"Thank you very much," and each of the three men, in turn, shook the hands of Agya Sei.

"Words alone are not deeds but a man's word is usually his bond. Thanks again," said Wofa Atta. As they said goodbye and stepped out to go, Abena entered the room.

"Wait for me here I will be back presently." Agya Sei saw the three men off, came back to Abena who had a chewing stick in her mouth. She split a tiny piece from the main stick and used it as a toothpick. As soon as Agya Sei entered the room, she asked,

"Isn't Boatemaa marrying you after all?"

"I am the one who is not marrying her," Agya Sei lied to see Abena's reaction.

"Oh is that so, gladness and sense suddenly are descending upon this house."

"Don't relish or savor on this statement because I was just lying. You are going to help buy things for this marriage for Boatemaa."

Abena suddenly had a throb in the heart. "Are you really marrying Boatemaa?"

"I have married her already because there's anticipated agreement from Papa Adjei's household."

When word got to Papa Adjei, he realized that Agya Sei was only putting on a bluff and that Boatemaa should have played a little hard-to-get also but there wasn't any need for further constraints so he accepted everything. They waited for Agya Sei.

The worst thing about local polygamy is that the old wife or wives are directly involved in the marriage proceedings of their husband's next wife. It was so in the case of Abena.

She took the insult of being the one to purchase bridal items which included imported Dutch wax cloth, shoes, necklaces and other trinkets, headgears, cosmetics and other toiletries. She reluctantly accepted her husband's money to buy the items.

"I will get Boatemaa's father to work on the necklaces and other trinkets as he is a goldsmith and being work for his own daughter, he will produce the very best for her," said Agya Sei.

"I don't care what you do with her, when do you expect all these?"

"As soon as possible."

Abena was going to tell her married daughter in Kumasi as soon as she got there. It surely will make a good conversational item for both of them. She had no doubts about her daughter's disapproval of the whole thing so she was determined to give her a piecemeal account.

In Kumasi, Akua demanded the reason for her mother's sudden visit and with her sharp sense of observation she noticed the melancholy and plaintiveness in her mother's frustrated eyes. She welcomed her and asked, "What brings you here today unannounced?"

"Haven't you heard the news?" She pretended to think that Akua knew about it.

"It's your father, he is marrying again!"

"What, who, when, how? !!!" Akua said with evident consternation.

"Yes, he says his new position as member of parliament requires a new wife. For this reason he is marrying an educated girl, Boatemaa, Papa Adjei's daughter."

'Incredible, she is only a fledgling. How can he sorely disappoint us by marrying again and on top of that to a small girl."

"Men have strange reasons for their decisions. Your father's main reason is education to go with his new role."

"Did he consult you at all?"

"Yes, he did."

"And you gave your consent without letting us know?"

"I had to."

"So I suppose it's too late to do anything about it to reverse the situation."

"Yes it is. In fact, my coming to Kumasi is mainly to solicit your help in purchasing things for the marriage."

"You are such a soft person to tolerate such nonsense. If it were myself he would never have peace as long as he remains a bigamist."

"What makes you think, I've left things as they are? Don't be surprised when things begin to fall apart. Also, I know more about your father lately and I don't fail to say that the marriage won't work."

"What is it, tell me, or I'm being too inquisitive."

"I guess so, but we all live to see. If you are not too busy why not go with me to town to make the purchases?"

"Not me, I can't be a servant to a person I am older than. What will she think about us. You can go alone, sorry."

Abena felt disappointed and useless but for the sake of her husband she would go to town. She took a bigger bag from Akua and left her after telling her she would be back. Her husband had particularly instructed her to buy "garment," the local name for Dutch wax, a type of good quality light material imported from Holland. She decided to go to the market women at the Kumasi Central Market. When she got there, the traders haggled over the prices of the cloth with Abena.

"It is five," said one lady, a bit thinner than Abena and with a thoroughly bleached face and dark body.

"What! Five million cedis is too much."

"What will you pay?"

"How about three five?"

"I don't even get the price I bought it for if I sold it for three million five hundred thousand. The last price is four eight. Take it or leave it."

Abena left in search of better prices. She noticed that at those exorbitant prices she wouldn't have enough to buy five 'garments' as Agya Sei expected so she made adjustments to buy four plus two cheaper local material. After a laborious search, she came upon one fat woman who would sell it at four million five hundred thousand cedis. She bought the four and also some of the locally made ones. If Boatemaa did not want them she could come to Kumasi herself to buy them, she thought. She returned to Akua's place for a short rest before she left to go back to the village.

"Akua, I got everything."

"Good for you. When does the new bride move in?"

"Oh no, she'll go to Accra with him."

"How about when he is home in the village. Where does she stay?" Akua stood up and adjusted and retired her cloth around her chest and sat down again.

"A man must be with his wife especially a new one," Akua said.

"Can't she stay with her folks?" Abena asked.

"What will happen if dada is no longer the member of parliament? It could happen anytime now that coup d'etats are a dozen a pesewa."

Abena was deliberately silent for a while as if thinking of a scheme for the inherent problem. When she was ready to go she got up not especially satisfied with herself.

When she got home, Agya Sei was deep in sleep quite susceptible to evil thoughts and machinations but she only waited one more hour till he woke up. For one thing, she loved her husband. Abena showed her purchases to him while she disclosed that the money was not sufficient for everything and therefore the necessary changes in some of the items bought. Agya Sei was choleric for a long time but Abena just ignored him. She was quite rightly saddened by her husband's ingratitude but she kept her emotions under control.

"I am going to seek the help of some elders in town when everything is ready to take them to Papa Adjei and his wife, and formally and customarily, ask her hand on my behalf. Akwasi's father can help with this," Agya Sei seemed content to say. "Boatemaa will be proud to see the chief himself under her father's roof," she said with some sarcasm.

"I think so too," not realizing her sarcasm.

In a matter of four days, Agya Sei gathered his friends around him. They were Agya Kwame Yeboah, Opanin Kwaku, Maame Akua and Auntie Akosua Nyarko. These were, of course, most respected personalities in the village. The two women carried the things in two big metal boxes and they set off on the way to Papa Adjei's house conversing heartily as if they were happy for Agya Sei. He, himself, needed restraint in order to conceal his extreme happiness. The little girl they had sent ahead to tell of their coming met them, on the way, and told them that Boatemaa's parents and herself were ready for them.

Papa Adjei was seated but immediately he saw the delegation he got one of his crutches and went to greet them. He thanked Agya Sei profusely for his diligence and Opanin Kwaku began to speak.

"I am happy to be one of the people to come and ask for your daughter's hand. Our elders have said that if a child knows how to wash his hand, he eats with the elders. Obviously, Boatemaa has shown some remarkable qualities that have attracted Agya Sei's attention." To Boatemaa he said. "Never let your beauty overcome you because after all, the beautiful woman owes her beauty and comeliness to her husband. Also, never be talkative about domestic affairs because a talkative woman reveals domestic secrets. As for you Agya Sei, I have three wives myself but it goes without saying that when a polygamist is ill he is usually starved to death. When many women are taking care of one man there are problems. I know it, well myself. I will entreat you to shoulder responsibilities equally," he said and seemed complacent with his admonitions. Agya Sei got permission from Papa Adjei and said, "Thank you, Opanin Kwaku for your wise words. To Boatemaa I will say this, "I know I am older but our elders have said that however beautiful a woman is, if she is divorced too often she loses the respect of men. I don't mean you are thinking of leaving even before the marriage is consummated, but, however great a woman is she is dependent on a man. I hope I am not being too general. I will strive hard to please you and love you as an experienced man . . ."

Papa Adjei interrupted Agya Sei and added these:

"When a girl is ushered into marriage she and her husband are one. During the marriage if she gains any good things they are for us the family but if she becomes bankrupt, gets in debt, and encounters misfortune then all the monetary responsibilities are on the husband." There was general laughter and small talk after which Opanin Kwaku asked if Boatemaa had something to say. She nodded in agreement.

"Thank you very much elders, for, it is because of me that you've gathered here tonight. I will take your wise words to sleep and think over. At my age, although I am going to be a mature woman, I only need to obey my elderly folk. I will try to be a good wife. Please, I beg you all, these are what I have to say."

When she said this, the trunks with her belongings were opened. She scrutinized with relish all that were present turning to show her mother from time to time some of the items. Agya Sei gave the "tirinsa" (bride price) of thirty million cedis to Papa Adjei and wife. He said that as soon as he could find residence in Accra, Boatemaa would join him. He also said that he would leave for Accra in three days.

Papa Adjei thanked Agya Sei and those gathered for the faith entrusted in his daughter. He said that he would take very good care of her while he was away finding a place in the capital city.

At Accra, Agya Sei was confronted with choices at Adabraka, Asylum Down, Ringway Estates and Airport residential area. He chose to settle at the four bedroom house at Ringway Estates. It was a plush place. Tropical ornamental trees lined the house. A well-cut hedge concealed this house from others around the area although it was easily accessible to the neighbors. The boy's quarters was separated from the main house between which a small compound was set. Unlike the village house, there was a lot of space. The garage symbolized the height of his endeavors for in it would be the Mercedes Benz which the government was going to give him. It was going to be a chauffeured Benz so he didn't need to go through the trouble of learning how to drive. The undisturbed tranquility and solitude that marked the place also heightened Agya Sei's achievement in a very big way. He was excited to inform Boatemaa and Abena of the place and even more anxious to bring Boatemaa to live there.

He went back to Kodie satisfied with what he had seen and accomplished at Accra. He gave himself and Boatemaa a week to pack up and leave for the capital.

CHAPTER 6

Only the other week, Boatemaa had come to be with her husband in the new environment. She was slowly learning the lessons of a wife and marriage and travel away from home. She had at least learned one important and worrisome thing about Agya Sei and maybe the marriage won't work as Abena told her daughter in Kumasi. It posed an albatross for her.

One day she joined Agya Sei at breakfast and asked,

"When do we get help from a houseboy?"

"I am making arrangements for one soon. The work has been tedious, hasn't it?"

"Please yes, I could use a houseboy to help in pounding fufu since you can't go a day without it."

"I see the problem, perhaps we shall get one through the watchman. He talks about a brother who needs work. By the way, why the need for a boy why not a maid?"

"I am afraid to have a maid because, as young as I am, I know the tricks of men especially when there is the question of a maid."

"But you know I haven't been able to do it lately. I am getting help from a doctor and another girl in the house won't be a problem. Your fears are not valid considering what you've learnt about me thus far."

After breakfast, Agya Sei went straight to the night watchman and put the request to him. The watchman promised to rendezvous his relative for the same evening when Agya Sei was back from work.

"I get good boy for you,' he said to Agya Sei. 'Nobody better pass my brother. With him for house, you go find results in no time," he said in broken English.

"How old is he?"

"He be sixteen and active, plenty."

"I think he will be young enough to obey my wife's supervision."

"Please, make you no worry about that. He be good boy."

That evening, the watchman brought his brother thirty minutes before Agya Sei arrived from work. The watchman introduced the brother as Salifu. He was a nice clean cut boy who looked strong and enthusiastic. He had a long scar on the right cheek from a tribal mark. He could speak Twi with a better accent than his brother. Agya Sei agreed to take and make him start the following day. He arranged Salifu's pay and conditions for work with the watchman.

How quick Agya Sei was to respond to Boatemaa's request. He knew his own shortcoming so to keep Boatemaa he was prepared to do whatever she asked him to do.

Agya Sei showed Salifu his living quarters. It was an easy evening for him as there was not much to do. The next morning, Boatemma swept the house and gave the garbage to Salifu to go to the dump. He saw to it that his employer's bath water was warm and ready. He ironed the pair of pants and shirt which Agya Sei had given him. The day was not very hectic for Salifu as he ran a few errands and pounded the day's fufu. The rest of his evening was spent with his brother in convivial and fraternal conversation. He seemed settled in already.

Later on, as the days went into weeks and weeks into months, Salifu easily became a liaison between Agya Sei's household and the neighbors. Matters leaked out of the house as if the neighbors were just eavesdropping and they became the source of gossipy conversation in the eyes of the Ringway Estates' neighborhood. For what reason they gossipped and were interested in Agya Sei's household was known only to them. They were just nosy and busybodies.

"Let me tell you something about our new neighbor and his daughter," the first neighbor said to the second.

"Who said she is his daughter? She is married to him if you don't know."

"Really, but how do you know?"

"Salifu our house-boy told our watchman. He and his brother are friends to our watchman and things come through them. He said she is his new bride."

"In my opinion she is young enough to be his daughter."

"I thought he was her grandfather," said the first neighbor and cackled.

"Some girls can be too money loving. How can such a marriage go on. I wonder if he can consummate the marriage at all. Ha! Ha! Ha!"

"I think she did the right thing. She will have plenty of money should he die soon," the second neighbor contributed and laughed heartily.

"You are right he is the new member of parliament and I hear money is next to nothing to him; at least, according to what Salifu tells our watchman."

"Where is he from?"

"They are both from a village close to Kumasi."

"You see he is a farmer according to sources.'

"He seems striking with all these qualifications but I don't like him. He is an "awengaa"(young girl lover). The next time you know it he'll be after your daughter."

"What! I would kill him if he tried," the first lady said, adjusted her cloth and retied it under her armpit. After much talk they went back to their houses.

With Boatemaa's help, Salifu kept the house spic and span and the little poultry of Agya Sei was bustling with vivacious life. Three hens had a clutch and one turkey had started laying. The poultry had easily become, in fact, the primary point in Salifu's existence in the house, a variable center around which most of his time revolved. He cleaned the coops everyday and fed the chickens and turkeys. He always lifted them by the wings to check their weight and, one day, he said to Boatemaa.

"You go have fine, fine Christmas because you no go need for spend thousand five for fat chicken. Wanna own dey do fine plenty."

"We don't have to wait till Christmas before we eat chicken because even in the village we had it often. Agya Sei will be pleased to have one soon.," she said and smiled at the boy's efforts, a bit unmindful of the current marital problem she was facing with Agya Sei.

"I get one rooster that I no go mind for kill. It make plenty trouble and fight plenty too."

"We can have it on the weekend, Agya Sei is expecting company and they would love to have chicken."

When Agya Sei came home, he informed Boatemaa of his visitors for the weekend. He revealed that plans for the building of his house in Kumasi would be discussed. Boatemaa remained exhilarated whenever Agya Sei mentioned the house. Perhaps, she could coax him into making her take care of it and eventually being the sole owner. She was always conscious of her husband's promise when he came to ask of her hand. Her enthusiasm to meet the deputy ministers was magnified.

On Saturday, the skies were clear and the humidity was lifted by a constant breeze. Four splendid looking Mercedes Benz sedans parked in front of Agya Sei's house. Boatemaa met them courteously and invited them to the house.

"I beg you, please, would you like something to drink?" she asked politely.

"I'll just take a glass of Pepsi Cola," one of the gentlemen said.

"Do you have any liquor? I could go for some whisky and coke," another man said.

'Yes please, I will bring them to you to make them yourself."

The other two men took a bottle of Star beer. Agya Sei came in from the bathroom, muttered something to his wife and sat down with his company. Boatemaa went to the kitchen.

"You have quite a young and pretty wife. How can you manage such a young one?" Mr. Dickson said.

"Thank you, we've been married not a year yet. I am glad you think she is good."

"She is too good for your bald pate. I don't think you deserve her." Mr. Nyarko teased and winked at his friends.

"What do you mean? Money and a good reputation alone can get you anyone you want regardless of age, I think. I was courageous enough to ask and she agreed. It didn't come so easily you know."

The five men drank and talked while the food was being cooked. They talked much about work at the top level and all agreed it was more tedious than anything they had done before. Agya Sei's ulterior motive for calling his friends for a visit surfaced when he asked Mr. Nyarko about cement allocation. Mr. Nyarko was directly in charge of Housing in government.

"There's no problem, you can always rely on me," Mr. Nyarko said.

Immediately Salifu came in to set the table, and shortly Boatemaa brought the food. She dished everybody's in big pyrex bowls and invited them to supper. Mr. Dickson dug in the food and commended Boatemaa right away. Agya Sei was feeling big in his head and was actually very proud of his wife. He was however, until now, not knowledgeable about how to please Boatemaa in the sexual way.

"This is the best opportunity for us to build a nice house. If we lose it, that's it for us," Agya Sei said.

"I agree with you." Mr. Dickson said.

"I started one before I was even elected but I didn't finish it because of lack of money," Mr. Asumadu said.

"If I had a wife like this I will never leave her," Mr. Nyarko said.

"I don't intend to," Agya Sei said.

As soon as Boatemaa left the room, Mr. Nyarko asked Agya Sei about his other wife and children.

"I don't need to think about them when I am enjoying Boatemaa's company."

"How does she keep up then?" asked Mr. Asumadu.

"Oh I remit them occasionally for her and the children's upkeep. But my wife Abena is very enterprising and always has money."

"What does she do?" asked Mr. Dickson.

"She is a hard working doughnut maker and akpeteshie seller in the evenings."

"Isn't she jealous when she sees a new younger woman sharing her husband?" asked Mr. Nyarko.

"I don't suppose so, after all, what can she do?"

"Don't be so sure, I am not polygamous but I know women. One woman is enough "trouble" let alone two or more," said Mr. Asumadu.

"Some women are full of jealousies, tricks and hatreds," said Mr. Dickson.

"I am not afraid of whatever happens. I believe I can get both wives under control."

They were interrupted by the sound of the telephone. Agya Sei excused himself and picked up the receiver. Meanwhile, Salifu, upon

Boatemaa's cue, came in to collect the plates and clean the dining table. Agya Sei came back from the phone and took his seat.

"When do you expect to start building?" Mr. Nyarko asked.

"As soon as possible, I have negotiated for land with our chief back home."

"Then, I will get a building contractor for you soon with all the necessary accoutrements for your house. How is that?"

"Just fine, thank you."

"It's getting late and we must go," said Mr. Dickson.

"I hope you enjoyed yourselves," said Agya Sei.

"Surely, we did."

They thanked Agya Sei and Boatemaa and each promised their host that they will see one another again through reciprocal invitation. Agya Sei saw them off and was happy about what went on.

After their guest left the house, Boatemaa informed Agya Sei that instead of staying home doing nothing except housework she could own a boutique and a hairdressing salon. Agya Sei thought the idea was good, however he felt bad that it wasn't his idea to begin with. He gave her a positive promise to do as she expected.

CHAPTER 7

Today, Agya Sei went to the urologist's office and told the doctor of his current problem. The doctor, noticing Agya Sei as the member of parliament felt some sympathy for him. He told Agya Sei that he would help him. He did a routine check-up and told him that, sometimes, age had a direct effect on low testosterone levels for men.

He said, after the physical check-up, that Agya Sei was strong and physically fit. Agya Sei was encouraged. The doctor didn't want to pry further into Agya Sei's family life so he did not ask him about his wife or wives. He wrote a prescription of Viagra (100 milligrams per tablet) tablets for his use. The doctor advised him that he should take one tablet one hour before intercourse. Immediately Agya Sei got home that night, he took one tablet before he ate and took a shower and waited for the hour to pass.

Agya Sei told Boatmemaa to do whatever she was doing quickly and come to bed in an hour's time. When they were ready, for some reason, the medication wasn't working. This posed a really big anxiety and embarrassment for Agya Sei. He decided to go back to the doctor the next day and he did.

Agya Sei took out a white handkerchief and wiped his furrowed brow which had begun to collect sweat on account of the stuffiness in the room. The doctor turned the fan on.

"You know, too much worry and fatigue can be factors for your current problem."

"Okay doctor, I understand but how can I stop worrying?"

"Turn your mind from this problem and try to do other things of interest."

"What things for example, doctor?"

"Don't you like sports?"

"I love it especially soccer, I am a Kotoko fan."

"Go to the sports stadium often. You can even take your wife along. Don't wait until Kotoko comes to Accra before you go to see a match. Many times, matches between Hearts of Oak, Olympics and other teams are just as interesting. I don't suppose it's only football that you like?"

"Oh, I like Horse racing as well."

"Well, go to the Turf Club too."

"Yes, but I've been going there. I like the betting."

"You can also take your wife to dances or to the restaurants."

"I like going to the restaurants better."

"Always relax yourself mentally and physically, exercise the body and even just take a walk. Take your wife to Labadi Beach. You can even take a ride to Biriwa or Elmina beaches as well."

"So you don't have another aphrodisiac drug for me?"

The doctor noticing that Agya Sei would try anything gave him some placebo tablets. Agya Sei was thankful again. The doctor charged Agya Sei a substantial amount of money. He tried to beat the price down but the doctor was as adamant as a rock and stood his ground. Agya Sei thought the doctor was too full of questions. For one thing, he hadn't come as a cracked-up for any psychoanalysis today but, anyway, his questions tended to ease the tension on Agya Sei. Agya Sei went home quite happy again that something was achieved and couldn't wait to try the new tablets.

When he was home, he didn't tell Boatemaa where he had been. He hid the new tablets and would surely surprise her this time of his renewed potency. He quickly took the placebo drugs and waited until the evening, all his mind on surprise, surprise again. Surprise indeed it was for Agya Sei because the so called magic drug did not work once again. When he tried again and again and nothing happened, he gave up and was inundated with anger, shame and disappointment.

"Where did the doctor get his education," he asked himself, very dejected indeed.

Agya Sei didn't give up the search for the panacea for his problem. He thought he should try traditional herbal medicine. He had in fact gone to the fetish priestess before not for this recent problem but the problem of one of his sick children, and things worked alright. "Why do I waste my time on western medicine," he thought. He knew a lot about the fetish priestess of the Akoma shrine so he went to her.

When Agya Sei got to the shrine and put forth what had been bothering him, the fetish priestess understood him and was quite sympathetic. She was a plump middle-aged woman who was neither beautiful nor ugly. She was a bit on the chunky side. One might say she was buxom the type of woman Ghanaian men liked. She was decked out in a white cloth which was wrapped over her breasts and under her armpits. Her hair was "mpesempese" (rasta). She fitted quite rightly into the local standards for a nice sexy lady. She recited some incantations and told Agya Sei of his problem even before he mentioned anything to her.

"How were you able to know my problem?"

"Don't be surprised. I have some powerful dwarfs who work for me. They told me of your problem as soon as you sat down."

"Can you help me then?"

"Yes, why not! Many men with similar and even worse problems have come here and were cured. Yours is not a problem at all."

"Really, then I think I am in the right place."

"Of course you are. You'll see black magic at work under your own eyes. What do you do anyway for work?"

"I am in government."

"If you'll agree to this one condition then I'll help you. After I am able to help you, you must first try it on me. Afterwards, I won't charge you anything but whatever you feel befits my help in the matter of gratitude for me will be appreciated. You can be witness to my power and send my name abroad to your big shots."

"Agreed! Agreed! Just help me and you'll see for yourself that I am not a worthless person when it comes to gift giving."

She gave Agya Sei some concoction of water and different herbs to take a bath with right there in her improvised bathroom. After that she gave a potion to him to drink and take the rest home and come back the next day after finishing drinking everything.

Agya Sei, carefully, followed the simple instructions and came back the next day. The priestess took him to her bedroom. Everything was nice and quite. Immediately she took off her cloth, bingo, he felt a strong stir in his loins. The drug had worked. After some practiced caresses of hers, Agya Sei felt strong and potent again and hit the sack with his magic worker. The resultant ecstasy of new potency filled Agya Sei with tremendous happiness. After the amorous session the fetish priestess told him of what to do with Boatemaa. He couldn't wait. He just couldn't wait!

Throughout the evening and supper, he fantasized about a good encounter with his young wife. He couldn't or just didn't want to eat much. He took a quick shower and called.

"Sister Boatemaa." Now it was Sister Boatemaa and not just Boatemaa.

"Yes, I beg you, I am coming."

When Boatemaa came in, he said rather bluntly, "Let's do it."

"Do what?"

"You get in bed and you'll see what."

"It's no use, you are going to get me all fired up and leave me cold."

"No, I say you'll see'. He was sure of it because he could feel an erection." She quickly undid herself and, true to God, a most fantastic evening of a belated encounter was in progress. It swept Boatemaa off her feet. She enjoyed it as never before.

Much later, Agya Sei bought a white ram together with ten million cedis to be given to the fetish priestess. Even much, much, later, Boatemaa revealed to Agya Sei that she had missed her period for close to three weeks and was sure of her pregnancy. With all the baffling problems he had had, Agya Sei seemed to have forgotten Abena and her children. With new relief for him, he thought that going back to Kodie was a fine idea. Afterall, he had something good to tell Papa Adjei and company and better still, start on his proposed building because on the way was the future heir apparent as he intended and called the yet to-be-born child knowing, and fully aware of his older male children with Abena.

"Why don't we go to Kodie this weekend?"

"I'd love to'" said Boatemaa said. They prepared for Friday afternoon, when they planned to leave for the village.

On Friday, the chauffeur took them first to Kumasi and then on to Kodie where they stopped at Papa Adjei's house so that Boatemaa could go and visit her parents.

Papa Adjei hopped on his one leg to meet his daughter and son-in-law.

"We thought you were never coming back."

"The work at Accra keeps us busy," Agya Sei explained.

Boatemaa's mother spoke up: "And how is life as a city woman?" She seemed eager to hear everything about Accra. Boatemaa smiled

"It's a more lively place than here, of course. Home is quiet, but then there's the sea shore, Makola market, the stadium and the race course. Shopping is easier because there are so many more shops than here in Kumasi."

"Ei, so you have seen the sea?"

"Yes."

'How was it the first time you saw it?'

"She was afraid to go near it. She also thought it was too noisy," Agya Sei cut in for Boatemaa.

"You are actually living it up with your new Mercedes Benz. You'll soon be the talk of the town." Agya Sei was ecstatic about Boatemaa's disclosure of the pregnancy and was just too happy to tell his in-laws.

"We are expecting a baby."

"I beg you. You should have let me tell them," Boatemaa cut in.

"Congratulations!" Papa Adjei and wife said almost simultaneously. "We shall be grandparents to a dignified and worthy grandson or granddaughter," the wife said.

"It's not only young men who can do it. You are still strong and virile Agya Sei," Papa Adjei said.

"Don't underestimate me or count me out yet. I am full of surprises." He knew definitely well that he shouldn't be over enthused about the whole thing because only God knew how hard he had worked at it. They were all hysterical.

Agya Sei excused himself to go and see his friend Akwasi and his father before going home to Abena. Akwasi was not at home but he had a good conversation with the chief who confirmed and told Agya Sei that he had got the plot of land near the Kumasi Sports Stadium for him.

"It will cost you thirty million cedis."

"Oho, you mean that little plot alone?" Agya Sei said rather surprised at what he had heard.

"Yes. Things are frightfully expensive these days. It is up to you in government to bring prices down."

"We'll do our very best. I shall go to Kumasi to inspect the plot of land and see if it's worth this big amount." As they talked on, Akwasi emerged and was surprised to see Agya Sei in his father's house.

"How have you b-been? I wasn't e-e-expecting you at all."

"I am fine but it's busy and quite hectic in Accra."

"Government w-workers are always c-c-complaining you c-can c-come here often f-f-for a visit. It's y-y-your hometown. Are you h-here about the land in K-Kumasi? My f-father has done the n-necessary . . . ."

"Yes, he just told me and I hope to be ready with the money soon because I want to start building. I don't want to waste time." Agya Sei was proud to say.

"I want to make it quick to impress Boatemaa."

"How is she?"

"She is fine and pregnant too."

"Ei, Agya Sei y-you'll k-kill us." He burst out singing the local tune to a happy marriage"

We wish you a happy marriage
A happy marriage we wish you
A happy marriage, A happy marriage
You and Boatemaa.

He switched the key of the song from falsetto to his natural and hoarse baritone.

"You and B-Boatemaa are quite p-pals now, but, how c-can you be s-so s-sure and trustful about this g-girl? I still th-think it's A-A-Abena who should g-get first choice a-at this. B-Boatemaa is very young. I warn you all about the l-loyalty now. She is wise. She is u-using her wisdom to-to get something from you."

"I don't believe so. She loves me."

"Fear wo-woman. Don't say I n-never s-said it. I think h-her glamor h-has blindfolded you. Do you think sh-she'll marry you t-till you die? I don't think s-so. She will s-surely find her way w-with some younger ch-chap somewhere. You must do something f-f-for Abena. You have m-m-many children with her and she l-loves and ne-needs you now. Your best b-bet lies with her I-I-I am telling you."

"You don't convince me. I know my wives better than you do. It is up to me to do what I think is right. I'll build for Boatemaa whether she is young or not. Again, I am confident that she loves me, ha."

"Ah, well said and done, but also take a good cue from my son," the Chief said. "Alright, Nana," Agya Sei said knowing too well that he wouldn't heed the Chief's advice. "By the way, when can we go for a drink? I will be here for three days."

"Whenever y-you are f-f-free, I will be ready, however if it s-sounds odd t-to you, do you th-think we should go and sit in-in the bar with all th-the people now that y-you have such a re-responsible position?"

"Don't worry, it's the work of a good politician to always mingle and stay in touch with the ordinary folk."

"If i-it doesn't b-bother you then it's al-alright with me."

"I must go and see Abena."

"You m-mean you haven't s-seen her since you came?"

"Not yet, why?"

"Ei, Agya Sei hmm!"

"Never mind I am going to see her right from here."

When he finally got home, Abena queried him about why he had kept so long in coming home from Accra and while he was in town.

"I have been with Boatemaa's family all this time," he lied purposely.

"How is she?" Abena asked as if she cared.

"She is fine and pregnant too," he smiled.

"At your age you are still having children; is he going to call you grandpa or what?"

"Don't be a smart aleck. I am performing my duty as a man and husband."

"I will say what I please; as you perform your duty as husband to one wife you are also consciously neglecting me and my children. Your youngest daughter had been very sick but we didn't hear anything from you after we wrote," Abena said with a louder-than-usual voice, yelling at her husband.

"The way you let somebody write, I didn't think it was very serious."

"But you knew she was admitted to the Okomfo Anokye Hospital; why are you so callous and uncaring now?" she yelled at him again.

Agya Sei was defeated by Abena's yelling and strong words, but he still insisted that he was not at fault. He asked where his daughter was and went to see her. She was all tears.

"Papa it had been a long time but why don't you care about us these days? Is it your new wife who is deliberately keeping you away from us? I was terribly sick."

"Darling, I care about you a lot."

"Then why?"

"Yes, I heard you were sick, do you feel better now?"

"Yes, I am better. But you should have seen me a couple of weeks ago. I thought I was completely gone."

"I am glad I bring you some comfort. I will leave you a good sum of money when I am leaving. Is that any consolation?"

"Yes, we need the money, but your presence means more. You knew there are some things money can't buy. We need to see you more often and a child's mind still tells me that you must divide your attention equally between your new wife and Auntie Abena."

"Well said, I always knew I had a precocious child. Thanks." As short as he was with his senior wife, he still had the itch to go out so he thought a drink with Akwasi won't be a bad idea. He thought so despite the fact that he had just left him. He sent Kwaku to go and call him.

When they were at the village bar, the owner and customers were full of approbation for his efforts for Kodie and the rest of the constituency. Some praised him for the new macadam road that replaced the old dangerously potholed dirt road. He was also praised for the new loans he managed to acquire for the local farmers.

"Give us a potful and two calabashes," Agya Sei said to Owuo, the barkeeper.

"They will be there shortly, please."

They sat down and took two quick drafts of the sweet sour liquid. After each calabashful Agya Sei swirled the remnants of dregs around and spluttered them on the ground. Some experienced drinkers could get a loud noise out of this ploy but with Agya Sei, despite his experience, his were smudged into no sound at all. 'You are n-no plam wine drinker', Akwasi teased and showed Agya Sei how to do it. After a successful, loud noise those sitting close by applauded him. His head swelled and he gave a long smile and said, "Domestic a-affairs are not l-like dirty li-linen which are washed and d-dried in public however let me s-say this b-because poverty does not appoint it's d-day of visitation.

A man's cir-circumstances or fortunes m-may s-suddenly change but be careful how y-you treat A-Abena. I always t-tell you this."

"If you are in love with my wife you can have her," Agya Sei said with a force evident in anger.

"We c-came here for f-fun. I didn't mean to s-start it all by making you an-angry. I am only s-sympathetic with her. That's all."

"Okay, Okay. You know politics is such a thankless job. Just think about what I am doing for the village and how others are criticizing me," he switched the conversation.

"No, they were p-praising you."

"I don't mean these people here," he said. "People are talking about my Mercedes Benz car and saying that I am using my position to enrich myself."

"Never m-m-mind them, I don't know of any p-politician who was n-never criticized. If they h-had the same o-opportunity they would d-do worse things."

"This Mercedes is not even mine. It's a government car. I am yet to buy my own."

"I am sure y-y-you can b-buy it too, politicians everywhere, I don't fail to s-say, are tricky and sometimes corrupt but b-build your house first." Akwasi took another swig, heaved a sigh and spat a fast and long spit. He filled his calabash and topped Agya Sei's for him. "Thanks."

"We n-need more D.D.T. for our ailing c-cocoa trees," Akwasi said.

"Oh yes, we've been discussing D.D.T. at our parliamentary proceedings lately and I have been made aware that it is a poison not so good for any environment."

"If it was n-not so good, why w-would people who make it c-c-continue to make it?' he said and took a slow draft. Some of the froth was attached to his moustache. 'Cocoa will s-suffer if this p-potent insecticide is e-eliminated."

"Well, for our cocoa's sakes, I am not going to vote for its total elimination, unless of course, we get a better more potent one."

"In m-my o-opinion there is no s-substitute for this in-insecticide. It works b-best against "akate" our cocoa disease a-and I am sure all the-the farmers in the country will raise a l-loud noise if it was v-voted out."

"I don't think it will be eliminated a while yet." Agya Sei swatted some flies from his empty calabash and poured himself a fresh fill. The pot was emptied by this act. Both finished their calabashes.

"I will pick you up at eight thirty to go to Asokwa I hope you don't mind."

"That's f-fine with me."

As a hearty political ploy Agya Sei shook hands with several of the customers before he departed with Akwasi.

The next morning at eight, the chauffeur got the car ready. He went to see if Boatemaa was also ready as Agya Sei had suddenly decided that she must go along too. They all went to Asokwa after they had picked up Boatemaa and Akwasi. Agya Sei was impressed to see magnificent buildings some of which were new and beautifully built. It will be a good neighborhood, he thought.

"I like our plot's nearness to the stadium," said Boatemaa. "Every local or international activity will be a stone's throw from us."

"H-How do you like it?" Akwasi asked as they got closer to the plot of land.

"Everything is good about it except the price but I can't let this opportunity go to another person. I will take it."

"Good," Akwasi said.

"Fantastic," Boatemaa said beaming a white smile.

Before they left for Kodie, they visited Akua, Agya Sei's married daughter. She was polite to them but she inwardly harbored some hatred for Boatemaa. Her hatred was obvious because somehow she had got to know of her father's proposed house and to whom it would belong after it was built. She took the cash gift that her father gave her without even thanking him.

Just before they left, the June clouds were thickening and blackening in the east. There were noisy thunderclaps, but they got home before it rained. The rain cleared the car of its dirt giving it a new sheen. Agya Sei spent almost all of the remaining time at Papa Adjei's house only to come back to Abena in the evening. Abena was noisily silent all the time to show to her husband that even though she was now getting little attention, all her time should be hers alone. Agya Sei inspected his farms and prepared to leave the next day.

CHAPTER 8

It was a hot, humid morning. People's head itched from the direct heat. The children of the village, almost wearing nothing, were in their numbers to wave goodbye as the flashy Mercedes pulled away from their houses.

"Did you have a good vacation?" Agya Sei asked Boatemaa to lure her into conversation.

"I beg you, yes."

"What was the best thing about your vacation?"

"It was good to see my parents and friends again. How was my in-law? I mean Auntie Abena your wife? She doesn't like our marriage too well does she?"

"She is doing fine. She is just full of jealousies. I can't understand. It seems to her that I am the first and only bigamist."

"Perhaps she thinks you give me too much attention."

"Yes, she thinks so but how can I help it. Your soup tastes better than hers. Her soup is like brine."

"Oh men, but you ate that brine for a very long time without complaining to her; now she doesn't know how to cook. Tomorrow, when you are tired of me, you'll tell me my soup is worse than brine as you say of Auntie Abena's soup, ei!"

"She is one jealous old hag."

"I beg you, don't say that about your own wife. Maybe when you get tired of me you'll say worse things."

"I'll never get tired of you." Boatemaa smiled into a long silence, laid back at the back seat where the blowing coolness of the breeze lulled her to sleep. Agya Sei did the same but was restless and stayed awake thinking deeply about something. He was thinking about Akwasi's assertion about the DDT and the ailing cocoa trees. If DDT was eliminated his cocoa would be wiped out due to the cocoa disease and he would have nothing to depend on. Definitely, he was going to lobby against the insecticide's elimination in parliament. He thought about other agenda including deliberations on the rights of children. He thought that, internationally, every child must have a right to education, not to mention food, shelter and clothing. He must have the right of freedom of expression. He thought that if such rights were lacking anywhere then, it was the duty of developed nations to help the children of the underdeveloped world. Parents should also carry their responsibilities squarely. He said this quite unmindful of his attitude towards Abena and children. Something broke his thoughts when the driver stopped briefly to urinate in the bush. Immediately, a flood of food peddlers surrounded the car with their goods.

"Yes, orange, two for twenty."

"Yes, bananas, three for ten."

"Yes, roasted plantain and nuts, ten, ten, ten."

Agya Sei was tickled and a bit amused at the peddlers' eagerness to sell their merchandise. Perhaps they were attracted by the Mercedes. Boatemaa woke up suddenly when she heard the noisy sellers.

"Do you want anything?" Agya Sei asked and pointed to the oranges.

'Yes, I could use some of the fruits, she said. She called one orange seller and bought fifty thousand cedis' worth. She gave one to Agya Sei and one to the driver who took them and began sucking at them. They were off in a moment.

There was a light shower when they arrived at the house at four o'clock in the afternoon. Boatemaa sent Salifu to buy some Ga kenkey and fried fish with steaming hot pepper. Agya Sei didn't like kenkey so Salifu bought him rice and stew and salad with eggs.

After supper, they lounged in their lovers' couch and waited until night fell indolently. At seven o'clock, darkness shrouded them menacingly and while there was nothing else to do they retired to bed. They slept for a long time and woke up suddenly from some snarling and constantly barking dogs, perhaps, on a mating spree. They were not able to coax themselves to sleep any longer. Agya Sei fantasized about lovemaking but put it off for a good reason known to himself.

Morning found the neighbors in a merry dialogue again. Their intermittent giggles reminded one of school girls. Sometimes, they turned into raucous laughter so much so that Boatemaa could hear them although she couldn't see them talking.

"Isn't Boatemaa pregnant by now?" The first neighbor said with a wink. An air puff, a bit strong, untied her headgear. She grabbed it quickly and retied it with a stronger knot.

"Are you kidding? I think all his steam is gone," the other neighbor said and laughed boisterously.

"You never know young women. While her husband is trying hard to make her pregnant, she might be already pregnant with some young lover. The pregnant woman alone knows the father of the baby she is carrying, our elders used to say.

"I see they are putting up a big kiosk. What are they up to now?"

"Salifu tells me she is learning hairdressing now and that the kiosk is her future hairdressing salon and boutique for hair products, and also foreign dresses."

"A big man like that with a hairdresser wife?"

"Don't be too surprised. It's becoming more and more glamorous now that there are perming, jelly curls and rasta. You see rich women with such hair styles these days. Even Makola women."

The two women's attention was distracted when the chauffeur came out with the car and stopped momentarily to take Agya Sei to work. When he was in full view the neighbors feigned a greeting to which he only responded lukewarmly. Perhaps he knew what they were talking about.

Agya Sei was not spiffy today. He had a cold and felt some chest congestion. He knew fully well the symptoms of his asthma and he knew he must stay home but, no, he was a "workaholic" so he must go to work. He went back into the house and took his oral inhaler just in case. When he came back, the two women were gone.

At parliament, the current topic on the agenda was cocoa and its rehabilitation. Agya Sei was feeling weak but he found a good opportunity to deliberate on the question of DDT. It was an intellectual discussion which revealed that the insecticide per se was not actually harmful to the cocoa trees but since it was water insoluble it tended to accumulate in ecosystems and had many toxic effects on a good deal of other vertebrates. Cocoa needs D.D.T. but the environment doesn't which one do we choose?" said one of the many farmers in the morning deliberations.

Cocoa is the country's mainstay so D.D.T. should definitely stay." Agya Sei said pounding his first on the table despite the fact that he felt weak.

"Yeah, we need D.D.T. for our cocoa." The Minister of Agriculture said and gave an overview that the insecticide had a direct bearing on the country's economy. If the country abandoned its use, surely, the economy would suffer, he said and made a motion to put the issue to vote. After further deliberations, the motion was seconded and voted upon. It was a unanimous yea for the insecticide's existence. D.D.T. stayed, thanks to Agya Sei and the Agriculture Minister. After the meeting, the Agriculture Minister came to Agya Sei who was having difficulty breathing. The minister helped him up and later told him of Agya Sei's recommendation to the President about a possible opening in his ministry. Agya Sei, as if by magic, felt better right away. He asked what the position would be and the Minister told him that it was that of a Deputy Minister. The thought of it enlivened Agya Sei to the point of much discussion with Mr. Dickson and Mr. Nyarko. In the evening, he could not wait to break the news to Boatemaa. She considered what this would-be position would bring to her image, her parents, Kodie and the whole constituency. It would be a lever for her husband's already dignified image in the eyes of his village. She prayed strongly for confirmation by the President. Three days later, Agya Sei was summoned to the President's office.

"The Minister of Agriculture has sent a recommendation for your appointment as his deputy. His recommendation is in accordance with whatever potential and capability he has seen in you. I myself think you have the strong qualities to take up this important and sensitive position and therefore accept the Minister's recommendation for your appointment." The President took his pipe and lit it. Agya Sei sat down to avoid the direction of the smoke.

"Thank you very much, Sir. I am much flattered by your confidence in me. I will do my best with the help of the secretaries to enhance, in a practical way, the already good image of the ministry."

"A reminder, this year we should see a bumper crop in foodstuffs and a good cocoa tonnage."

"You definitely will. Thank you again."

Boatemaa was joyous by Agya Sei's news of his new appointment.

"Our constituency will be glad to know this," she said to Agya Sei and was full of renewed admiration for him. She meditated on how, further, she would get on the better side of her husband. Her behavior from now on must be exquisite, she thought, in much overenjoyment.

"With this appointment our building in Kumasi will go faster because there will be more money," Agya Sei told her as he relished on his new achievement. The news just called for a little toast. Boatemaa brought one of Agya Sei's stock of Jack Daniel's and some soda. She fixed a glass for her husband and she took the rest of the soda, as liquor, she said, was very loathesome.

"Cheers to success," said Boatamaa.

"Cheers to a good year for us," they clinked glasses. He took the whisky straight and chased it down with the soda. He imbibed some more, more and more that he had become intoxicated without realizing it. Surely, whisky was not palmwine which one could drink almost a potful and walk straight home without the least staggering. Agya Sei went to bed to sleep off the booze.

Boatemaa inspected again her big tummy and knew the day was closing in. She prepared herself mentally and emotionally for it. Being her first time, she was a bit nervous as many women had told her how painful childbirth is. "Such things are inevitable for women. It is almost like having one's period, the first time," she thought. She sat for a long time in heavy thought. She felt lazy and leaned against the wall about to doze off when the telephone rang. She let it ring two times before she got up to take the receiver.

CHAPTER 9

How soon nine months come around. Boatemaa was in the hospital. Her delivery had been prolonged by a longer than usual labor. She had been worn weary to the point of tears.

The nurse midwife was very calm though and knew the baby would be out soon. Agya Sei was waiting anxiously at the V.I.P. lounge and pacing erratically all over the place. When the nurse came out briefly, he thought everything was over but he was told that the doctor wanted him to be by the side of his wife to help her through delivery. He immediately obliged and went in with her. Soon after Agya Sei's presence, the baby's head appeared. Boatemaa was encouraged to push with all her might. She did and, in a flash, the baby was out. The blood nauseated Agya Sei. It was a robust baby boy who responded to the doctor's slap with a sharp piercing cry. All was well. Boatemaa felt limp and dwindled. She stayed in the hospital in a day's rest and came back home with the baby. A week after that they gave the Twi name of Kwame Wusu Nkwantabisa to the boy. Boatemaa wanted Stephen for a baptismal name so Agya Sei named him Stephen Osei during his baptism a week later.

News had reached Kodie already and Papa Adjei and wife travelled to Accra to see their grandson. Boatemaa's mother agreed to stay back and help out for at least a month.

Salifu was busier now that the baby had arrived. He always got the house spotless for he was aware of the type of people who came to visit the family. Agya Sei rewarded Salifu for his efforts.

Important personages came in their numbers to visit Nkwantabisa. Among them was the President's wife. They brought different kinds of gifts and money. The baby had easily become one pampered celebrity.

The neighbors found a fresh item of gossip since they were always nosy and busybodies.

"She had a boy," the first neighbor said.

"Yes, I hear Boatemaa's mother is here."

"How about Agya Sei's other wife. We've never seen her here. She should rather be careful before Agya Sei bequeaths everything to Boatemaa now that she has a boy."

"I wouldn't be surprised. He seemed not very concerned with this wife in the village. If I were in her shoes things would be different because one doesn't buy a cock and let it crow in another man's village. She has labored too much with this man to just let a young girl take over," the first neighbor said as if Boatemaa didn't deserve anything of her husband's.

"I've heard she doesn't even take her rivalry with Boatemaa to the extreme. Salifu says she brought gifts to the baby. It's like carrying the gun to your murderer."

"Come off it, it's not with her that her rivalry must show. It is the husband whom she should show much disdain."

"Actually she is helpless to the situation. I feel sorry for her, don't you?"

"I do too."

"Agya Sei is shirking responsibility to this poor woman, I wish she comes here. We shall tell her what to do."

"'Ei, let's not meddle in other people's family affairs."

"Yes we shouldn't measure the depth of the river with our feet. That is we shouldn't run unnecessary risks. We are just neighbors." Immediately they saw Boatemaa, they dispersed, scurrying like frightened mice.

Boatemaa was learning the joys and sorrows of motherhood. She cleaned after him, washed him and carried him on her back every time she fed him. She was very fond of the boy because she knew he would bring her luck. The only thing she didn't like was his constant crying at night but since Agya Sei was always ready with a helping hand, she was not too fatigued during the day. With all the careful attention Nkwantabisa burgeoned into a very healthy infant.

When he was six months old, mother and father took him to his hometown where family and friends came to wish him welcome to a village which his father had helped put on the political map of the country. Everybody, especially Boatemaa's friends, wanted to take turns carrying the baby but as he was not used to them he always cried.

Agya Sei went to Asokwa to see the progress of his building. He was satisfied with what he saw and upon confirmation by the building contractor, he learned that the first floor could be completed in two months.

"I will make sure to pay one visit a month to acquaint myself with the house's progress."

"That will be good motivation for the workers," the contractor said.

"How long will it be before the whole building is completed?"

"Give me five months and it will be ready to be lived in."

Agya Sei was exulting in his fait-accompli. Pretty soon, Boatemaa and Nkwantabisa will have a whole house to themselves. He got to Kodie in time to see Akwasi to whom he related his child's birth and progress on the building. Akwasi was impressed by his friend's new fame and happenings in his household. This time, Akwasi was quiet about the plight of Abena for he knew Agya Sei had gone so far in his dedication to Boatemaa that changing his mind would be like cutting an iron rod with straw.

Abena had lately been thinking of how she could get even with her husband. She wished him every evil even though death was not a better panacea for him for his conscious negligence of her and her children. She knew she must do something and do it quick too but she couldn't think of exactly what. A thought came to her finally.

"I will go to the Agoro fetish and put a curse on him perhaps, he will learn a lesson from it," she said aloud to herself smiled malignantly. She knew her children would corroborate with her. Even if none did, Akua in Kumasi would, surely, be with her in carrying out the decision. She was richly filled with the happiness her cogitations had brought.

When Agya Sei got home he brusquely asked for his food.

"If you really wanted food why didn't you go to your other wife? After all, everything of hers tastes better."

"Don't insult Boatemaa, he warned, "or you will get it tonight."

Abena curled her lip and said, "What will I get? You couldn't beat a chicken."

He wagged a finger in her face and screamed, "Be careful, I warn you."

Abena backed away. She grabbed a machete off the table. "Be careful of what?" she screamed. "If you so much as touch me, you will see whether your blood is yellow or green!" She brandished the machete.

Agya Sei overcome with cowardice, didn't mention a word and went inside, too angry to eat. He preferred to sleep hungry rather than kowtow to a quarrelsome wife. The silence was poignant between them until the next day. In the morning, Agya Sei had occasion to reconcile with his wife but he was not interested. Instead, still angry, he took a bath and left to go to his other wife's place for some tender loving care.

Agya Sei had not even said goodbye to Abena. He was ready to leave for Accra with Boatemaa. Boatemaa took her time in getting ready.

Agya Sei was getting tired of waiting because he knew he must be at the Sports Stadium in time to witness the grand durbar of chiefs which was a magnificent gathering of Ashanti chiefs in their beautiful kente cloths and gleaming real gold necklaces, bracelets and other trinklets. At this durbar, there was a lot of drumming and dancing.

"Perhaps you can wait here and take more time getting ready. I will go to the stadium and pick you up later."

"Please, I beg you, can't you wait a little for me to finish. It won't take any longer now. I want to see the durbar too."

He yielded to his wife's tardiness although it was beginning to be uncomfortable for him. Finally, she and Nkwantabisa were ready and without any delay they took off for the stadium. There, it was a sight to see. Chiefs had arrived in their numbers. They were resplendent in their gleaming kente and gold ornaments in the form of rings, necklaces and headgear. The Asantehene himself was there in all pomp and pageantry. He had arrived in a palanquin carried on the shoulders by several stout men. He held a golden staff with which he danced to the melodious drums behind him.

In majestic glamor, the golden stool, the soul of the Ashanti Kingdom, was displayed while chiefs and subchiefs were introduced amidst drumming and dancing. When all the dignitaries were seated, the Asantehene gave a general historical overview of the reason for the gathering. Agya Sei knew a lot of the history behind this. He had learned a lot from Akwasi's father who was also present in the gathering, so he was not at a loss at what the Asantehene said. But Boatemaa kept running with a myriad questions. Of course, she was very young.

"Is it actually true that this Golden Stool was commanded from the heavens by a fetish priest as they always claim?" She asked after a moment of contemplatively regarding the famed stool.

"Yes it is true. History has it that the priest was called Okomfo Anokye who, in the historical past, and at a gathering similar to this, commanded the stool from the heavens to come and rest at the feet of Osei Tutu the then chief of the whole Ashanti Kingdom," Agya Sei contributed.

"I find it hard to believe the miraculous magical powers of this fetish priest, but I will go for its mysterious credibility just like any other Ashanti." The most important thing is the tradition that goes with it. It is symbolic of the unity of the Ashanti people," he said. "However much difficult it is to distinguish truth from fiction, it is established that Okomfo Anokye, by his magical powers brought this stool to supply the religious basis of the Ashanti Union." Boatemaa nodded her head in accordance and admiration at her husband's knowledge of history.

The august ceremony lasted until late afternoon when Agya Sei and company left to go to Accra. On the way, little Nkwantabisa cried nervously, fatigued by the activities of the day. Sometimes, Agya Sei's anger at the non-stop crying of the child was evident in the spanking he gave the boy. Boatemaa was infuriated at him for beating the child. At Nkawkaw however, little Nkwantabisa was soothed to a coca cola refreshment upon which he kept quiet.

"I think he is running a temperature," she said with concern.

"He is sweating profusely. I agree he is sick. Let's see the doctor as soon as we get home." She took the child from him and tried to coax him to sleep, and was able to pat him lightly to sleep. Agya Sei had an overwhelming desire to smile as he looked at the sweat beaded forehead of the sleeping child and the sudden tranquility. He was full of gratifying appreciation for Boatemaa. "No doubt about it little Nkwantabisa had malaria," the doctor disclosed when Boatemaa took him there after they had been in the house briefly. The doctor gave her some Paracetamel and quinine tablets and took a million cedis from her after the nurse injected the little boy with chloroquine. He cried.

The following day, little Nkwantabisa was well. Not having much to do Agya Sei called some friends to go to the turf club. Agya Sei had heard about the new sensation in the horse races so he intended to gamble and bet heavily on Ponko Pa," because he was quite sure of winning considering the winning streak of that horse lately.

There were three races today, and when they got there, the first race was about to start. The jockeys and their horses were at the line up. Meanwhile, Agya Sei had gone for some bets, but this time not too heavy ones. He was anxiously waiting for the last race in which "Ponko Pa" would race. The signal went for the start of the race and everything was honky-dory. At the last stretch Agya Sei was surprised to see that he was winning. His horse came first so he collected his wins which amounted to twenty million cedis. His friends advised him that that was enough money for the day so he should quit gambling. Agya Sei, however, didn't pay attention to them. He went ahead to bet on "Ponko Pa" at the last race and lost thirty million cedis in the process. He went home dejected.

"I should have kept my first wins," he said.

CHAPTER 10

It was a strange time in Abena's life, full of silence and wondering how to put her life back together. Inevitably, her situation touched her children. They were well aware of the tension between their parents with the sure instinct of the young and they reacted taking sides with their mother. Akwasi had found much occasion to be empathetic with Abena to the point of paying her visits now and then in the absence of his friend.

"Your s-s-silent attitude these d-days reflects some kind of di-discordance with Agya Sei I can t-tell; anything the matter between you and him?" He asked soberly and concerned.

"We are not on talking terms," she said with a melancholy stare in her look.

"What happened?"

"We had a fight when he was here and that resulted in our cold war. Actually, I started it all but I wasn't at fault. He puts his other wife before me while he deliberately allows our relationship to be pejorative," she said and cupped her hand under her chin.

"What have you done to remedy the situation?"

"What can I do, he has gone to the extent of building her a house. I was so dismayed in utter disappointment when somehow I found it out and truly, I am burning with hatred out of contempt for him and his wife," she said with a definite tone of resentment.

Akwasi knew for a fact that the substance of her world was disintegrating and it was the fault of his friend. He felt like taking her out of her usual surroundings, telling her and convincing her that everything would be alright. She deserved to hear it from him he thought.

Abena, on the other hand was appreciative of Akwasi for trying to bring some balance and direction in her life once again. Maybe there will still be time to salvage her marriage. She relished his friendship and looked forward to his subsequent visits. He proved to be a true consolation for her unsteady psychological make-up and circumstance.

Boatemaa had been very calm and loyal to Agya Sei and he seemed to trust her, however, what he failed to realize was her consuming attitude; she was never satisfied, always reaching avidly for something she considered more important, more befitting of her hungers and aspiration. She had no patience for the content and compliant. She had long discerned that her husband was a big sucker so she hit on this weakness hard. It was even more appropriate for her to use little Nkwantabisa as a good excuse for making demands. The house was nearing completion and legal matters had been underway for entrusting it to the sole possession of Boatemaa and child.

Hardly had this been finished, when she made demands for a new car. Agya Sei, as experienced as he was, was however unaccustomed to what she could beef up again and again to get the better side of him. He came home to an unusually ready woman in all aspects. She always looked her sensual best and her still firm and pouting body was persuasively gratifying to her prey. One night her flaming sex appeal lured him to a very rare and satisfying-beyond-words sexual encounter. And in the process her ulterior motive became apparent. She said,

"Won't it be exquisite and rather glamorous for a minister's wife to have her own car?"

"You dummy, you think I live for you?" he said with sudden anger.

"What! I beg you, what did you say?"

"You heard me," Agya Sei seemed serious.

"Is that so, then I am ready to pack off."

"It's in your own interest if you leave. You'll lose the building as well."

"Why have you turned like this all of a sudden?"

"Don't think I am a sucker. I always want to do things on my own initiative. I don't want to be told everything." Agya Sei's mature age asserted itself.

Boatemaa was taken aback. Her surprise suddenly turned into heart throbbing of fear. He never acted like this before. Is there another woman I should have known better because what he could do to Auntie Abena, he can also do to me." She was set a-wondering. Agya Sei broke her wondering thoughts by saying;

"The building contractor tells me of a finished building in two months."

"Do you still want to give the house to me?"

"I promised you that didn't I? What I am sure about myself is the ability to keep promises. I promised you and your parents so you'll have it."

"I beg you, thanks. From now on I will always wait for you to say whatever good things you want for me and Nkwantabisa."

"Won't you have a housewarming party?"

"I had it in mind but I was afraid to ask."

"Well think about it."

"I beg you, alright." She was now condescending. "I can go back to the village earlier to see to the preparation before this important event," she said with a readiness that was distantly filled with eagerness. She planned for a big party.

At home, she informed her parents that the building in her name would soon be finished and she had come to seek ideas on how best a party could be organized.

"We can all help," her mother said excitedly as she took little Nkwantabisa from her.

"I have an idea, I am sure he'll come with some friends so how about a catering service?" Boatemaa said.

"Yes, why not get Asco restaurant at Asokwa to do most of the work. They can bring nicely prepared fried rice and stew with garnish, meat pies and steaming kebabs right to the house. Agya Sei will get his friends at the Brewery in Ahensan to bring some cartons of beer and I myself will see to the minerals and soda beverages."

"That sounds like a good idea but when will he be here?"

"By the month's end he'll be here, perhaps even sooner, it depends."

She paused and then continued. "He would round up his friends and as soon as he can, he'll be here."

A week into the next month, Agya Sei arrived with Mr. Dickson, Mr. Nyarko, Mr. Assiedu and Mr. Owusu. Their eminent presence highlighted Boatemaa's importance, an importance which she took the greatest care in nurturing with discriminating essence.

The next day was Saturday. It was a bit overcast. Cottony clouds moved across the face of the sun and the place was all cool and cool. The coolness became even more pronounced as the trees and leaves swayed back and forth by the constantly blowing breezes. All was correct and honky-dory. The caterers brought their victuals and good cheer. There were invitations to Akwasi and his father. Overall, there were thirty five people in the house. Although, Agya Sei invited Abena and children they were conspicuously absent.

Akwasi's father's linguist poured the libation invoking the ancestral spirits to come and drink. He asked for lasting prosperity for everyone, children for the childless and better health for the sick. He thanked them for this favorable afternoon and all the people, some of whose affluence (affluence attributed to the grace of the gods and dead spirits) was shown in the magnificent building. He poured a little bit of the glass of schnapps on the ground and guzzled the rest. He squeezed his face and heaved a sigh. After this, Agya Sei got up and said,

"We are blessed that we can gather here this afternoon under your auspices to this merriment. We thank you and we'll continue to bless you gods and dead spirits. Always come to our aid when we call on you and never find fault with us because we don't give you drinks often. It is for the sake of my wife and child that we are gathered here and in a symbolic way, I hand over the keys of the house to her."

Boatemaa stood up maturely, nurturing her top level experience from Accra. She moved to the side of Agya Sei. She was clothed in a blue patterned "garment" some of which she used for an elaborate headgear. She was twenty one but she looked thirty five by her fullness in the cloth and camisole.

"Dear husband and guests," she said and paused a bit. "It is truly an honor this afternoon to be standing by you to receive this precious gift in appreciation of myself and our child. Over these three years, he hasn't promised and failed. That I know for a fact. It is the mark of a true husband and for that much I am most grateful. I also promise to be a very good, loyal, and faithful wife." The guests clapped uproariously and Boatemaa and husband exchanged a few confidences while the hub-bub continued. After it died down she said,

"I especially requested a song to dance to our success. It is a highlife record and you can join in after we introduce the floor."

The disc jockey reeled a melodious record in Akan. Agya Sei held Boatemaa for a "smooching" but she broke away to display her expertise at the highlife dance. She was crisp in her steps and her occasional circling was a delight to see. Everyone felt a dancing sensation by watching her. They tapped the floor and slowly, one after the other, joined in. The merriment of eating, drinking, dancing and small talk had begun. All was well. The spicy and aromatic khebabs combined with a pleasant sense of smell with a delightful sense of taste. They ate and imbibed the liquor as if the food cost nothing.

Agya Sei was a clumsy dancer. It seemed his bandy legs were always in the way as he kept stepping on Boatemaa's feet. He danced to the first song and sat down to drink and watch. Boatemaa had lost all discretion, she was too carried away by the dancing that she was rather sensual in dancing the with younger men. A rather jealous Agya Sei called her attention to it right away and warned her. He and Akwasi drank while they became inebriated but their self control was impeccable, these two experienced drinkers. They drank on. The felicity of Papa Adjei and wife defied all others. The music was good and even Papa Adjei got on his crutches to the floor and bogeyed down. Merriment lasted into the night. After the merrymaking, those who wanted to go home did so. Those who couldn't, stayed over and slept. It was everybody's first time.

They slept for a very long time but Boatemaa got up early to attend church service at St. Peter's Cathedral. There, she thanked the good Christian Lord for his abundant Providence and favor. When she came back, she joined in the clean-up. After much cleaning, she took a closer look at the house and its aura impressed her a great deal. It was painted all white with blue trimmings. It consisted of four apartments; two at the bottom and two at the top. The railings were painted black and all the doors were clear azure. There were paneling in all the rooms. The floors were tiled. They nonetheless had linoleum carpeting except for the halls of the top apartments which had woolen carpeting. A wall surrounded the building to conceal ample space in front, part of which was planted with bougainvillea. The rest of the space was cemented. The building contractor had deliberately left two big mango trees at the back. These provided ample shade and a person could delight in a repose in a hammock slung between the lower branches. One would think Boatemaa would be very complacent now but she wasn't satisfied. Something was missing but she now feared to make another request to, sometimes, upredictable Agya Sei.

"I will ask, come what may," she said.

CHAPTER 11

Abena was overwhelmed with joyous gratitude when Akwasi paid her a visit. Akwasi was fascinated by her calm attitude and composure. She got up at the break of dawn and fried her doughnuts. By about seven thirty, fine brown doughnuts were ready for sale. She was almost always able to sell everything but some of the village folk liked to buy on credit too.

She offered Akwasi a chair and three nicely browned doughnuts. It was too early to distinguish any kind of romantic affection between the two. Had Agya Sei learned of the motives of Akwasi he would have been very incredulous about the impending God-forsaken affair and come back quickly to his wife.

"Why d-don't you p-pay me a visit a-at my house?" He asked Abena who couldn't conceal her surprise.

"For what?"

"Come and you'll s-see. There are things that c-can't be said inf-front of everybody."

"Don't you think we are too old for this?" Abena asked as if she knew what Akwasi was about.

"I know we have all p-passed our prime b-but nothing is t-too late to start again. We h-have established f-friendships that need to b-be fortified if w-we are going to g-get anywhere at all."

"Ei, so you are "bossing" me."

"Well, i-if you th-think so, yes."

"Then, when do you want me to come and see you?"

"How about s-seven o'clock on T-Tuesday evening?'

"I will make time to come."

Akwasi had succeeded in getting her to agree to pay him a visit but would she come really? That was the question. However, contrary to Akwasi's apprehensiveness, Abena showed up on Tuesday evening. There was a bright half moon in the sky, the stars were twinkling and everything was in line with romance. The room was large according to village standards. Although there was no electricity, Akwasi had a fridge and a fan. White elephants! A long partition concealed the "secret" place where the bed was. There were four "airtights" also.

"Why are you single, if I may ask? Didn't you marry before?" Abena asked.

"That is a b-belated question. I was n-never fully married . . . ."

"What do you mean you were never fully married? A person is married or not married. What happened to you?"

"I had p-proposed to ma-marry one Akosua Donkor however, since I didn't have much money at the t-time to pay her brideprice she left me. Women! Hmmm!

"Doesn't the lonesomeness get to you? I've experienced what it is to be lonesome after that darned elections. Hmmm," Abena said with a heavy sigh.

"It's n-no l-l-longer lonesomeness when two l-lonely p-people meet. We c-can turn our situation a-around for a better one. I will be t-trully good to you if you agree to be a b-better and t-true f-friend.

"I know what you are getting at but what will your friend think when he finds out?"

"How is h-he going to f-find out? He is t-too busy with Boatemaa to p-pay any attention to you. That m-m-must say something to-to you that he is m-moving away from you. I-I think he feels like d-dumping you and you don't s-see it."

Abena was silent as if lost in thought. She knew exactly what Akwasi was saying but perhaps for fear of thinking about it she had relegated it completely. She was forty-five years old and a faithful wife, the only man she had known was Agya Sei and the prospects of a new relationship baffled her tremendously.

She said, "I still love him."

"Don't be f-foolish, don't you know p-p-polygamy makes a man d-deceitful? A man with five wives has five tongues."

"So the chief is deceitful eh?"

"In m-marriage, I-I guess so."

"Well."

"Well what? When the hunter is r-ready with its aim, the bird is th-thinking about where it will p-perch."

"I will think about it."

"Well and good. When c-c-can you come here again." Akwasi asked with apprehension again.

"Anytime, afterall he is not here, ha, ha!" Abena said and cackled.

"Your feeling is m-mutual."

"Let's make it a clandestine affair."

"You've g-got it."

When she came to him on Friday, Akwasi was more aggressive and succeeded in sealing their friendship with mutual intercourse. She was quite embarrassed afterwards for being unfaithful.

"You don't h-have to be embarrassed, y-you are not a s-small girl."

"Won't you feel guilty if you were a woman and you disappointed your husband for the first time?"

"If he is t-treating me right, I will feel a-ashamed and guilty but not w-when he makes me f-feel unwanted," he said and put his cloth on and came out of the partition. Meanwhile, Abena made the bed and put her clothes on to join him. She took the basket, with which she said she was going to the market from the center table and placed it by her side.

"Do you f-feel like going already?"

"No, no I just took the basket away from my view. I couldn't see your pictures clearly. Is this Akosua Donkor?"

"Yes she-she is. I treasure the p-picture as it is the only one I have of h-her."

"Do you think of her at all? Where will she be, you think?"

"I used to th-think about her all the t-time but not anymore. She and her p-parents left to go to the nor-northern part of the c-country to sell yams. Probably, she i-i-is married to some Alhaji now. Abena smiled at the sound of Alhaji and said:

"Women surely like where money is. It is so true. Just think of Boatemaa. She is young, she hasn't seen much life yet."

"As for m-me the one I feel sorry f-for is Agya Sei. If anything should go wrong he will t-take a heavy b-burnt."

"I would feel sorry for him too after all you succeeded in breaking his wife's loyalty," her smile widened. He returned her smile and said,

"Maybe one d-day, I will not j-just be sharing a friend's wife s-secretly, we will be each others."

Akwasi had persuaded himself that he alone was responsible for everything between him and Abena and he did not regret it at all. All he wanted to see was some happiness for two people, who by no fault of theirs, were subjected to disgust of life. His action, he thought, would bring up their own drooping spirits. The Ashantis and Fantis always say that the bug that will sting you comes from your own cloth.

Abena used the excuse of going to market to visit Akwasi quite frequently. Nobody suspected any kind of misconduct yet as the friendship of Agya Sei and Akwasi was common knowledge to all.

Except Wofa Atta who had cause to suspect one day, when he saw the two valentines at a questionable place in the village. Will he tell Agya Sei? His evidence thus far was very small but he was going to keep an eye on the two.

At Accra, Agya Sei had been unusually late for work, quite uncharacteristic of him. On arrival, his secretary gave him a note which she said had been sent by the President. The note read:

"Mr. Osei, please see me immediately for an important information."

Agya Sei didn't wait one minute but proceeded quickly to the President's office. He got there while the President was out briefly. The secretary gave him a seat in the very plush, cozy and cool comfort of the office. The intensity of his excitement and anxiety brought some cold sweat on his face and hands.

"What could it be?" He picked a Daily Graphic newspaper to browse through. He dispelled any misconduct because to him, he had been constant at work without iniquity and had never missed a day yet. Well, he realized he was late this morning, partly not his fault. He glanced through the newspaper not necessarily interested in what the pages offered. He looked at his watch again and again and knew he had waited for more than ten minutes. He looked restless. He got up briefly to try to stifle the uneasiness on his mind. While at it, he was relieved by the President's voice beyond the door. He took a white handkerchief to wipe the sweat on his forehead. When the President came to Agya Sei he greeted him with a hard and vigorous handshake.

"Good to see you, take a seat and feel at home."

"Thank you Sir."

The President took a sheet from a file and sat down. "I have something to share with you because I appreciate your attitude to work." He handed Agya Sei the sheet. He took it, heaved a big sigh of relief and read it.

"It is about a conference which I want you to lead a delegation," he distracted Agya Sei's attention momentarily. "Actually there are two: one in Geneva and the other in New York. The conference is on international price of cocoa for producer countries. Which one do you want to attend?"

"New York, Sir, I have heard a lot about this great city and it will be quite intriguing to be in America whose people were able to put men on the moon."

"You are welcome to lead the delegation to New York then. Everything for you and your wife is at public expense and I will let you know the details of your trip soon."

Agya Sei didn't know what to think. He was ecstatic. Once again, his hardwork has brought him luck. All of a sudden, his cheerfulness was too much for words. When he got home he picked up Nkwantabisa and threw him up and caught him again in mid-air three times out of sheer elatedness. He told Boatemaa about it and she couldn't conceal her extreme joy.

Agya Sei and the rest of the delegation were given orientation about almost everything American including their typical food items—the hamburger, hot-dog, and apple pie. All the passports and entry visas were ready. Just the possession of a passport was a big joy for Boatemaa. Back in her school days when it became the fad of the day for most people to have a passport she had struggled unsuccessfully to obtain one. She had even lost "kalabule" (bribe) money in the process. She cherished this opportunity heartily and was full of appreciation for her husband whose tenacity at work had been able to bring that about. She savored the idea that humble Boatemaa was going to be a "been-to". "Maybe before I come back from America I will be speaking slangs too," she thought.

Finally, the day of departure arrived. Some government officials And reporters rendezvouzed at Kotoka International Airport to see their Minister, his wife and the other delegates off to the United States of America. A reporter asked Agya Sei of what he thought about the western domination in the pricing of the Ghanaian mainstay even though all of the raw materials for the finished products of chocolate, candy and cocoa butter came from Ghana.

"Why not get all the cocoa producers together and try to create a major embargo like the Arabs did with their oil?" One female reporter asked Agya Sei.

Agya Sei hesitated a bit and said nonchalantly, "Actually an embargo of cocoa won't be much felt by the consumers. If the consumers decide not to buy, what happens next. It's a compromise that we have to strike with them and, certainly, it must be mutual between the producer and consumer countries. I hope I drive my point home."

"Yes, but international buyers have no right to dictate the price to the producers," the reporter said as if to heckle the minister. Agya Sei only said, 'I am sorry', and turned his attention to the delegation. They picked up their carry-on luggage and made for the plane that was waiting patiently for them. The unusually long flight was uneventful but it was made a bit exciting for Agya Sei and Boatemaa, both novices at flying, by the constant musical interludes and film show. Whereas Boatemaa was delightfully enjoying the meals, Agya Sei even had the retching urge because he was not accustomed to the food on the plane. He stopped eating and drank more.

"You are going to the white man's land and you should learn how to eat his food," Boatemaa said and crunched on a small celery and zucchini although it seemed she didn't like them.

"Who said America is a white man's country? It is also home for many Black Americans. Didn't you study about the Negroes in school?"

"Yes, we know Michael Jackson and Donna Summer. My impressions about Black America go to music, sports and the Peace Corps. I don't know of any really prominent Black."

"Come to think of it, there are not many big black men. Didn't you know the American President now is black. He is Barack Obama, some of our former American ambassadors were black too. Don't worry about who is big or not. I am sure we shall meet some prominent blacks in New York," Agya Sei said of course, he knew.

A little after the last movie, the plane jolted them with descent. The pilot announced that they were in the vicinity of New York City. He reminded everyone of the procedures for landing and before long, after he spoke, Boatemaa who had the window seat said,

"Look!" she said this revealing her up-country upbringing. Agya Sei moved closer to the window and also said,

"Look at the beautiful string of lights. How marvelous."

"Oh, the lights are so beautiful but I wished we had arrived earlier so that we could see the skyscrapers from above."

"You've got a whole two weeks to see them," Agya Sei said as he pointed to the well-lit Statue of Liberty.

Descent was gradual and jerky. The tarmac suddenly welcomed the acceleration of the Pam Am plane with care. Pretty soon, all was well and safe as the plane taxied to a complete stop at the entrance of the Pam Am lobby. After they had gone through Customs, they were met by the Ghanaian representative of their consulate in New York. He escorted them into parked cars outside Kennedy-Airport. Boatemaa couldn't believe the immensity of the airport compared to the one at home. She looked with mouth agape and was quite comparable to a hick who had suddenly been taken out of her element and placed in downtown New York.

"This is what we call an international airport."

"Exactly, I can appreciate how technologically advanced these people are."

They all continued to look outside at the landscape and environment which were lit up by fluorescent, incandescent and neon lights.

The cars sped by the huge buildings until they came to the Hilton Hotel. Their reservation was already there and the whole delegation was impressed by the dainty American hospitality. Their rooms were spotless. Boatemaa turned the color television on. She made a big deal out of the programs to Agya Sei who was fascinated by the excellence, typical of the Americans.

The next morning, Agya Sei met the Ghanaian representative again who took him and the others around New York city. They toured the United Nations Building, Empire State Building, Rockyfeller Plaza, the Statue of Liberty, Yankee Stadium and Madison Square Garden. When they finally got back to the hotel, they were worn to the bone with fatigue. They got ready for supper at the exquisite cafeteria at the Hilton. They relished the savory pork chops and baked potato with sauce. After reading the menu for the third time Boatemaa called for apple pie and vanilla ice cream. Agya Sei also took the same item and yes they enjoyed it. They also had a green daiquiri each for a drink. After the meal, Agya Sei and Boatemaa returned to their room where he prepared steadily for the conference the next day. Other members of the delegation came to him for last minute briefing.

The conference began at exactly nine o'clock in the morning. Representatives from Switzerland, England, United States, Brazil, Nigeria and Cote d'Ivoire were present in their elegant suits and traditional clothes. There was much deliberation about the glut of cocoa on the international market. Agya Sei insisted that there should be a cut in productivity until the glut was contained. A Swiss delegate wanted prices cut to expedite the purchasing from the producers. This aroused discontentment from the producers. A Brazilian delegate reflected on the much precariousness of economies of the producer countries if the price of cocoa had to go down further. There was a deadlock at the meeting that day and it was adjourned until the following day. Delegates mingled freely in seemingly trivial conversation. Representatives of big corporations like Nestle' and Cadbury were lobbying hard among producer nations but these nations realizing the massive profits of the corporations stood to their guns.

Agya Sei had departed with a Nigerian and an Ivorian delegate to a small post conference meeting in preparation for the resumption of the conference the next day. He returned to his hotel room to find Boatemaa fast asleep with the television on and the Soap operas running. When she got up finally, she was surprised to find Agya Sei home already.

"How was the conference?"

"It went well for a while but—"

"Is it over?" She didn't let Agya Sei finish his sentence.

"Not yet, we still have tomorrow."

In the morning, Agya Sei donned an immaculately grey suit with a spotted tie in a neat knot and sported an elegant executive portfolio. He strutted majestically in front of his delegation and took the seats reserved for the Ghanaians. The deliberations went on for a long time and when it was over everybody was satisfied with the developments. After the conference, Agya Sei and Boatemaa had some time for shopping. Their shopping spree took them to a car dealer. Boatemaa's insistence that Agya Sei buy a Porsche fell flat. Agya Sei had his eyes on a Mercedes Benz 450 SL convertible and bought it. Arrangements were made to ship the car as soon as possible so as to arrive at Tema harbor early. Agya Sei, on the advice of Boatemaa, bought some insignificant souvenirs to give to Abena.

As fast as the trip had begun so it ended. The day of departure sneaked on them. Boatemaa wore some suggestively tight body hugging jeans and a red top. Her face was elaborately done with eye shadow and blush. Her ear rings were unusually large and she wore some dangerously pointed high heeled shoes.

Surprising how only a couple of weeks could change a once modest country girl.

"You look like a prostitute," Agya Sei said pointing at her high heels.

"Ah, you surprise me. You call your own wife a prostitute! You should rather be commending me. If you don't have anything better to say don't say anything."

"You can't follow me with this to Ghana."

"What has become of you, your age has made you an "atetekwaa" (a hick). If I had married a younger man he would surely appreciate this." She was sobbing unceasingly and blew her nose every now and then.

"Yes, I am an "atetekwaa." You knew it and married me. If you don't change this funny appearance I will leave you here in New York."

"I dare you to leave me here."

"You are becoming—"

"I am not becoming anything. I am wearing this appearance if you like it or not."

Was Agya Sei also important here too? He was not able to control his wife and he felt useless again. That was to be expected because there was still a true lover's knot in his attachment to his wife. With glaring looks everywhere, they arrived at Kotoka Airport where the funny looks didn't cease. Agya Sei was full of embarrassment. At one point her shoes almost made her fall had it not been for the timely help of a delegate. When they got back, the delegation submitted a joint report to the President. Agya Sei was vociferous about their achievement which impressed the President a great deal. He engaged Agya Sei in conversation on his impressions about travel abroad and New York city.

"It's a good experience. In my opinion everybody should see America at least once in his or her lifetime," he said. "These people are too advanced; their highways, strong and magnificent bridges spanning non-polluted rivers and the amazing apparent cleanliness are issues for long discussions," he pointed and gave the President a sourvenir of the Statue of Liberty.

"England is almost the same although, I believe, modern America shows a better advancement in almost everything except, of course, purity and originality of culture. The place is a melting pot and you know different people make a good country," the President said and puffed his piped which briefly showed the reddish flame.

"It could be true. However, I don't believe it in our case because our tribal diversity and the heterogeneity of our cultures don't help us much when it comes to development."

"It took a long time before Rome was built my dear friend." The President said and lit his pipe which was flameless now, with a lighter. When he had caused a big coil of smoke to dangle in front of him, he exhaled and said with abundant jet streams of smoke from his mouth and nostrils.

"Thank you for your efforts on the country's behalf. They speak well of your sincere patriotism and commitment to the party."

"You are much, much, welcome Sir. Always at your service and the country's."

"See you."

"Thanks." Agya Sei left with much elation.

CHAPTER 12

The convertible hadn't arrived yet but despite her surprising and rather execrable behavior of late, Boatemaa was able to convince her husband that she wanted to learn how to drive in anticipation of the car's arrival. Agya Sei, what can he do, instructed the chauffeur of her desire and that he should make time especially on weekends to take her out driving.

The chauffeur, in a very short time, alleviated her apprehensiveness and brought her to the state where she could change gears comfortably. She was not afraid to step on the accelerator and she seemed to have great confidence in her teacher. She was exhilarated not only because she knew she could drive now but because she knew, by her usual way, she could twist the arm of Agya Sei to own the car too. She learned earnestly what she had to know about the theory and practice of driving. They had earlier practiced in a large open field where she drove flawlessly around.

Today the chauffeur took her on the road. She did a magnificent job despite the heavy traffic.

"I still have to drive alone to prove to myself that, in fact, I can drive."

"You'll have the opportunity but it's too early yet," the chauffeur said laughing. Just then a tro-tro driver tried to overtake them. She felt insulted because a rickety old lorry was going to overtake a Mercedes so she stepped on the gas and zoomed dangerously ahead. A car from the opposite direction was also speeding forward. An accident seemed imminent. Immediately, all of a sudden, Boatemaa instinctively stepped on the brakes to a screeching stop in the middle of the road. The oncoming driver had anticipated this and had also slowed to a stop. She was a bit shaken and didn't want to drive any longer so at the junction ahead, she traded her driver's seat for the passenger seat. The chauffeur gladly took it and drove flawlessly home.

A month after their arrival from abroad, the car arrived at Tema harbor and driven home. The effect of the presence of the Mercedes brought Boatemaa's life to a climax. Every morning, she dressed flamboyantly and relieved the chauffeur of his duties to drive her husband to his office. She seemed to show off the blue black Benz each time she got home because she would honk the horn to awaken the attention of the neighbors. Sure enough, after her fourth day, the neighbors were engaged in another gossip.

"Have you seen and heard Boatemaa? The fatter neighbor said.

"Who hasn't? She is driving now and in a new car too."

"Salifu said she went abroad with her husband." The fat neighbor said again.

"It surely did her good. She looks fairer and she has gained a little weight. Oh how I wish I were in her shoes."

"Be content with what you have. There is a lot of woes which are attendant to prosperity. I would like to see where this couple will be if they are unfortunate enough that the country encounters another coup d'etat."

"I think a coup will create havoc for them." The neighbor said.

"Don't you think she'll leave him if that should happen?"

"Ah you can say that again. I know for a fact that we shall outlive them in these precincts. After that, he would have realized where he should have buttered his bread. Boatemaa or his senior wife."

Two months had gone by with Boatemaa and Agya Sei not seeing much of Nkwantabisa. He was with his grandparents at the house in Kumasi. She missed him a lot and desired to have him back with them. She left with the chauffeur to Kumasi taking turns at the driving. Her excessive interest to drive the last kilometers to Kumasi and then on home stemmed from the fact that she wanted to impress her parents in a grand way. When she got closer to her house she looked in the rear mirror to see if everything was ship-shape. After she crossed the road towards the entrance of the house, she honked the horn three times. Her mother, with little Nkwantabisa, fast asleep on her back, came to open the gate. Obviously, she was surprised to see her daughter in the driver's seat.

"You know how to drive?"

"Yes," she smiled with a sense of pleasure not unmixed with personal achievement.

"Do you have a new car or this is for the government too?"

"It's ours, we bought it on our trip to America."

"Oh, how was the whiteman's country? Even if I don't have any more glories and achievements before I die, I will be satisfied because, after all, no other person than my own daughter has gone abroad to America. That's a big achievement in a lifetime."

Boatemaa looked at her son's face and hurried past the rooms to use the bathroom. Meanwhile, her father came out while her mother took the child from her back and placed him in bed. The loud conversation of Papa Adjei woke Nkwantabisa and he started to cry. Boatemaa came out and took him before her mother or father could get to him.

"Our daughter drives now," her mother told Papa Adjei with a smile.

"Is that true Boatemaa?"

"Yes, it is. I just started."

"Our daughter is becoming highly complicated now. Firstly, she has been abroad. Secondly, she drives a Mercedes as your mother tells me. We are proud of you."

"Thank you but I think I am a product of sheer luck. Agya Sei thinks superbly of me for that reason he gives me everything I ask of him."

"Be grateful to him," her mother said and sat on the couch.

Only one highly disagreeable task lay before her now—the courage to take Abena's presents to her face to face. Not that she feared her. She didn't want to infuriate her with her adeptness at driving and with the new flashy Mercedes. She might ask a little too many questions. She, therefore, drove to a friend's house the next day and, with some tinge of youthful courage, walked towards Abena's house and confronted her. Abena was surprised at her husband's other wife's unannounced presence.

"Welcome home," she said and looked for a seat for Boatemaa.

"Thank you." Boatemaa took the seat. To her surprise, Abena was already treating her like a queen. She asked her news from Accra and America and Boatemaa narrated an elaborated story. Abena sat quietly for a moment and her silence was broken when Boatemaa brought out the cheap jewelry purchased for her from New York.

"I beg you. This is from your husband, a gift from the foreign land."

"Thank you but where is he?"

"I beg you. He is a very busy man now. He said he would come home as soon as he has some more time." Boatemaa thought she was imagining the fastidiousness of Auntie Abena but as she could see Auntie Abena's attitude was really genuine. According to Abena, she didn't have a fight with Boatemaa. Agya Sei was the real culprit and she planned steadfastly to avenge all her misfortune. She was clearly sad and was, as the Ashantis would say, sobbing inside." Somehow, after Boatemaa left Abena's place, Akwasi learned of the blue black Mercedes that had come to Kodie. He also got to know through some garrulous elements in the village of his friend's other wife's presence. Immediately, he went to Abena and related to her of the new car. Abena had always wanted to be at Accra to spend some time with her husband.

"Is there any impropriety at riding with her to Accra?" She asked as she offered Akwasi a glass of water. Akwasi took the water from her, sat down and said, "I-I-I don't s-see anything wron-wrong with it. If I-I were you I-I-I would go to Asokwa tomorrow t-to enquire of Boatemaa's de-departure to the c-capital. It's a wife's right to-to be with her-her husband. As you c-can see she is wi-with him always and she g-g-gets everything. She is also we-well aware of your evil t-treatment too."

"Yes if one of two persons suffers or is ill-treated the other learns her lessons from such sufferings. Boatemaa, who is now the recipient of many good things will undoubtedly leave him in the event of trouble and hardship? She is too young to waste her time on a man who is almost out of steam."

"I-I can't imagine how Agya Sei c-c-can be so insensitive and fu-full of follies. Anyway, I-I agree with your-your going there with h-her when she leaves."

Abena's foot dragging made her miss the voyage. Boatemaa had left the next morning with her son and the chauffeur for the capital. Abena was unrelenting. Her strong determination to go to her husband characterized her preparation the day after. She went to say goodbye to Akwasi and left to take the Neoplan bus to Accra. She got there at two o'clock in the afternoon and asked her way from a taxi driver to the house at Ringway where Boatemaa was diligently preparing the evening meal. Obviously, Boatemaa couldn't contain her astonishment when she saw Auntie Abena. She gave Auntie Abena a glass of water and took her bag.

When Boatemaa took her to the living room she immediately saw a sharp contrast between their place at Kodie and this one. Her superficial acquaintance with the opulence she had guessed of her husband left her all of a sudden. She saw a big refrigerator and deep-freezer, luxuriously stuffed couches and a Davenports, woolen Persian carpets, a video deck and color television, a stereo with huge speakers and two telephones. To top it all, it seemed there was winter in the room for a humming air conditioner steadily super cooled the room in contrast to the heat and high humidity outside. She casually opened the refrigerator and freezer and found cold drinks, frozen fish and meat, and assorted vegetables.

"Wow! These people are truly living it up." She closed the fridge with a slight bang and went to sit on one of the couches. She felt and tested again the softness of the couch with her hands and rear end. When she saw the big color three family picture of Agya Sei, Boatemaa and Nkwantabis, a her jealousy and anger rose to a different boiling point. She stealthily went into the bedroom and discovered Boatemaa's tardiness at housekeeping that day. The room was very disorganized. There was even another television and telephone in this bedroom. To spite Boatemaa this time, she took the bed covers, made the bed and arranged everything to put a better order in the room. When Boatemaa finally came in, and discovered what Auntie Abena had done she was embarrassed and ashamed. She felt insulted but remained calm. Meanwhile, Agya Sei was working late in the office. He was well over an hour past his supper time. His senior wife's conspicuous presence annoyed him because Abena didn't give him prior notice of her coming.

"What brings you here?" He asked after loosening his tie knot.

"Don't ask me what brings me here. Am I not your wife and isn't a wife supposed to be with her husband. I am tired of Kodie so I came here to be with you for a while."

"You should have at least let somebody call or write me."

"I don't think it was necessary. After all what am I, a stranger?"

There was certainly some awkwardness in the direction of the conversation. He went to the bedroom to change clothes. Boatemaa had already set the table but he didn't eat right away. He attended to Abena and formally asked her "amanee" (news that a visitor brings). She said she had been in Kodie for too long and since through his own hardheartedness he hadn't invited her once ever since he and Boatemaa came to the capital, she found it necessary to take the initiative to come. Moreover, she hadn't seen him since he returned from abroad, consequently and obviously, she missed him. Agya Sei nonchalantly narrated briefly affairs at Accra and, of course, about his trip.

It was after supper and the inevitable sinister night was fast approaching with menacing darkness. It seemed the night smelled trouble already. It was a question of decision for Agya Sei. He must decide who should sleep with him. The idea of an orgy was out completely. Of course, none of the wives would yield to such highly absurd idea. His choice was not random. He was constant in his choice of Boatemaa. Upon learning about this, Abena was infuriated. She primed herself for a quarrel and possibly a fight. Like rolling thunder, she roared at her husband.

"Who did you say is sleeping with you? Are you nuts?" Abena words, grotesque in its unfamiliarity, produced a gust of anger in him.

"Who is nuts?" His right hand accompanied his words with a boisterous slap. Abena slapped him back and made for his groin anticipating to wreak havoc to the testicles which women, as well as men knew obviously well that they were the residence of sharp pain. Agya Sei, with his sharp reflexes, kicked a hard one and she was thrown back momentarily. She got up and grabbed the water bottle ready to hit the husband. He ducked at her throw and the bottle crashed against the wall. When Boatemaa heard this, she rushed inside because she sensed trouble. Immediately and upon instinct, she got Abena in a lock and wrestled her down. Abena was a bit wearied but surprising how Boatemaa was able to down a woman of Abena's size.

"Get off me, you slut," Abena yelled as she tried to pull herself from Boatemaa. As she successfully did so, she flung Boatemaa whose head hit the corner of the dining table. She was bruised and the sharp pain made her cry.

"You can team up with him, I don't care I will still fight." She twisted her cloth tighter around her waist and charged at Boatemaa.

"Stop your foolishness. Are you crazy?" Agya Sei uttered forcedly.

"You'll have to kill me tonight."

Meanwhile, Boatemaa dodged the charge timely and got closer to her husband. She was obviously panic-stricken. She pleaded with Auntie Abena to stop the fight. Agya Sei also pleaded because his initial enthusiasm at the fight had deserted him and replaced by a cowardly fear. His heart started to race.

"You started it and you'll finish it. Are you and your wife cowards now? "Tweiaa", you are not a man." She blew her nose loudly with the corner of her cloth.

"Please, I beg you, there is no need to continue. It will attract unwanted elements here and we'll all be embarrassed."

"I want both of you to be embarrassed. Shame! Ignominious shame!" She clapped her hands as she said this. She adjusted her cloth and suddenly sat down which surprised and relieved Agya Sei and Boatemaa greatly. Abena was sobbing unceasingly. She was like a child who had cried her heart out and needed to be consoled.

Agya Sei was relieved with incredulity when Abena sat down. He regretted not having repressed his fury to begin with. He moved closer to Abena and said, "You can sleep with me tonight."

"I will sleep right here in the living room and get away from me before I re-enact the whole scene. I am leaving here tomorrow as a matter of fact." She stood up with a jerk and made for the door, got out and banged it with a loud, irrepressible noise. Her indignation was uncontrollable. Agya Sei followed to try and make terms with her but she was not ready for them. She sat outside in the crescent moonlit night for a long time. The constantly blowing cool breeze made her shiver but she still sat outside to continue her self-imposed exile from Agya Sei and Boatemaa. Not long after the lull, her husband came out again to plead with her to go in and sleep. She sat for about ten minutes and finally went in. She took some of the cushions from one couch and improvised a bed along the wall facing her. Boatemaa brought her a pillow and a blanket but she only ignored them and drew her cover cloth over her face to coerce what turned out to be a restless and nightmarish sleep. She woke up and was impatient to see the brightness of dawn but morning never seemed to come. Her decision to leave, come dawn, was unbending. She switched the light on and began to pack. When morning came she took her bag and set for the station. Agya Sei and Boatemaa's incessant pleas and begging were useless. Agya Sei even ordered his chauffeur to take her to the station but she refused. She got a taxi and off she was at the station at nine a.m. and in Kumasi at two o'clock in the afternoon. Agya Sei was left a rather shamefaced and confused man.

CHAPTER 13

Boatemaa was a Catholic. She went to a Catholic high school, St. Louis Secondary School in Kumasi and she baptized Nkwantabisa at Holy Spirit Cathedral in Accra as stated before. However, she had always thoght that she was in an unChristian marriage. This time, she wanted to see things right.

She had a birthday party for Nkwantabisa. The highlight of this birthday was not the party the previous day but the church service that followed. Boatemaa had asked Agya Sei before hand that it would be appropriate to take their son to church especially on the occasion of his birthday. Agya Sei gave it considerable thought and yielded. It will be the first time in many forgotten years that he will go to church and he was not particularly anxious to do it. He was not a very religious man in the Christian way. Why does Boatemaa want Agya Sei to go to church?

"Which church do we take our son?"

"Mine of course. We are going to Holy Spirit Cathedral."

"I'll be out of my element there."

"Don't worry. I shall always be there to help out. I'll let you in on some simple rubrics like sitting, standing and kneeling."

"Do you actually have to kneel?"

"Yes, it's a most devout and humble way to pray to God. It's commonplace of us and it's not punishment to kneel reverently for the one who created you we believe."

"Do your priests kneel too?"

"They do much standing and genuflect every once in a while."

"Talking about priests it's in your church that they are celibates isn't it?"

"Yes."

"Do you think they keep this hard to take vow?"

"Yes they do."

"I don't think so."

"Why don't you?"

"Because, to me men are polygamous by nature and doing without even one wife is a serious handicap."

"I think men are just lusty." Agya Sei was getting more and more interested.

"Do you think perhaps some do indulge clandestinely in these sexual practices they've vowed against?"

"I am not saying they are all infallible as the Pope but I won't put down my church and religion by saying yes."

"It will be a serious vice to do what one has vowed against especially if it concerns something as sacrosanct as religion."

"God helps them to maintain it. You know the priests pray a lot."

"I still have my doubts."

"Okay you are entitled to your opinions, but let's get some sleep and go to church tomorrow."

Agya Sei switched the air conditioner on. It was one of those muggy nights when mosquitoes took the deliberate and adventurous liberty of causing irritation to people.

In church the next day, they were ushered into one of the front pews close to the altar. The choir sang hymns to help the priest on with the "Asperges me!" When the holy water sprinkled an Agya Sei, Boatemaa and Nkwantabisa, she crossed herself. Agya Sei also feigned a sign.

Agya Sei saw a couple seated in front of the aisle close to the altar and asked why they were there.

"Obviously they are going to be wedded."

"Aren't they too old to be newlyweds?"

"It doesn't matter. In this country, a couple can marry in the traditional way first and then later bless the marriage in a sometimes belated Christian wedding."

They stood for the Kyrie. At the Epistle and Gospel all the readings reflected the matrimonial essence.

They said that a man or woman will one day desert his or her parents to join a wife or a husband as one flesh and body. They also said that in the beginning God created Adam and Eve as man and wife and thus the marriage institution was an old and profound and sacred one that would last through generations as long as Homo sapiens existed on earth. They didn't say a man and a man or a woman and woman would one day get married and become one.

Actually, if one takes God out of the equation, because some people would say one is a God freak, it's only wise man out of all Nature's creation that think it's right to do so. It is a modern phenomenon. Marriage between a man and woman is an old phenomenon, so if there is a new phenomenon, they should come up with their new word such as "man-man union" or "woman-woman union" and not marriage. Marriage is sacrosant. Man-man union and woman-woman union are not Don't kid yourself. One day, somebody will wake up and say he is going to marry a spruce tree and he or she must be given his or her rights. I know that day is coming.

After much counseling during the sermon, the Priest came down from the altar to the couple and adhered to procedures for a wedding. The Priest said to the bridegroom: 'I, Stephen Odoi Mantey, I take Felicia Naa Korkoi Armah as my truly wedded wife . . . .' The groom responded after each sentence by the Priest. Likewise the man, the bride responded to the Priest the same words as had been given to the groom. After each of them had said their promise of 'For better for worse', they exchanged rings. The priest said, I formally declare you husband and wife in the name of the Father, the Son and the Holy Spirit. Instead of kissing, the couple hugged each other and the Priest blessed them with Holy water. The rest of the mass continued. During communion, Agya Sei saw many people going to receive the host but Boatemaa kept sitting.

"Why aren't you partaking in it?" he asked.

"I can't."

"Why not?"

"Because I am not married in church and all that I do is regarded as adultery in the eyes of God and the church. It is even more serious to be married to a bigamist. Someday, I want to receive communion as the others."

"In that case, I am putting you in perpetual sin because one, I am married to Abena also and second, I haven't wedded you in church."

"Exactly." Boatemaa's main motive for bringing Agya Sei to church was slowly asserting itself. She wanted to make a point and she was doing well thus far. When communion was over, they sat to hear the announcements. That added another half-an-hour to the already long service. Agya Sei was impatient to leave. Boatemaa realized this and said:

"I beg you, it will be over soon. We ought to get the Priest's blessings."

Not long after this, the announcements came to an end and the Priest got up and intoned:

"The Lord be with you."

"And also with you."

"May the almighty God bless you in the name of the Father and of the Son and of the Holy Spirit. The mass is ended, go and love one another."

"Amen." The congregation stood while the Priests and the acolytes, together with the long line of choristers, amid solemn singing, walked down the aisle. Boatemaa picked up Nkwantabisa and they were anonymous among the big number of congregation. They came out to find the chauffeur gone for a while. During their wait, Boatemaa tried to inveigle Agya Sei about the conversation that had preceded the end of the service.

"Tradition allows our men to be polygamous but in truth and in God's eyes, it is wrong. Christianity demands one man one wife," she said with calm composure.

"What are you trying to get at?"

"I am saying that it is wrong to be married to an already married man."

"So you want out of it?" The question was loaded with apprehension.

"Not exactly."

"What do you mean then?"

Boatemaa hesitated as if her next response might blow up the world.

"You don't care too much about Auntie Abena anyway, why don't you leave her and marry me in church. I'll be your only and truly married wife. In God's eyes you'll be blessed with copious forgiveness."

Agya Sei was taken aback by her bluntness. He said, "But that's a serious thing you are bringing up. How can I destroy a twenty five year old marriage in one day?"

"You can if you truly love me."

"Now, but that's a challenge. You know very well that I don't go to church."

"There's a beginning for everything. You've even started today." The chauffeur pulled up and apologized vehemently for his unruly behavior. Agya Sei as confused as he was by Boatemaa's inveigling attitude didn't say much to the chauffeur. Moreover, he had just come out of church and he knew a harsh reprimand would be inappropriate.

When they got home Boatemaa still brought up the idea.

"It will be right in the eyes of God, I tell you."

"God doesn't want injustice and leaving a long standing wife will also be sin against him."

"But in the Bible, Paul said a man should take only one wife, don't you think you'll be finally going in accordance with his teachings."

"But Abena is dependent on me."

"She can seek dependence elsewhere."

"At her age?"

"Yes. Haven't you seen the market women? She can be like one of them. All you'll have to do is give her a big cash sum which she can use as capital for some trading business."

"I am in a big dilemma," Agya Sei said.

"You shouldn't be. I tell you a wedding between us will take you away from your ungodliness. Moreover, you show more appreciation and love for me than for Auntie Abena."

"Yes, my love for her is waning, however, I still think she deserves my financial support from time to time."

"Don't you love me and want to become a man of God?"

"Yes."

"Why this long argument then?"

"It's only that your beliefs are unjustified. It is right for our custom to permit multiple marriages not necessarily for lust as your church and many people think but it is also for charity and magnanimity. If women who are unfortunate not to have a husband and are struggling in life, let's take the case of a widow with say six children, don't you think it is generosity when an already married and wealthy man offers to help by proposing marriage to her? Does God forbid kindness?"

"Kindness to women leads to affection, affection leads to love, love leads to lust and lust leads to adultery." Agya Sei was surprised at Boatemaa's intellect at the argument and saw the validity of her assertion.

"God said husbands love your wives. If you don't love Auntie Abena you are wasting her precious time and sinning grievously. I still think you should leave her."

"Let me think more about it. Maybe I'll have one or two discussions with my friends."

"No, let this be your own decision. Your maturity warrants it," Boatemaa said for fear that his friends might influence him the wrong way. Agya Sei wanted to yield to Boatemaa's request, however, he also thought it was wrong for a husband to destroy a relationship no matter how deteriorated it had become so dilemma, dilemma, dilemma! Traditional custom is not sympathetic with divorce and he knew it but, also, as long as he remained a very important person he still needed the very good and glamorous presence of Boatemaa to put some measure of elegance in his personality and position as a member of parliament and Deputy Minister. He was respected not only for his position as a member of parliament, Deputy Minister but for the ability to win and keep this young and beautiful Boatemaa so again dilemma, dilemma, dilemma!

CHAPTER 14

Abena could have gone straight to her daughter's house but she didn't. Instead, she took a taxi cab and headed for the village. The weather was inclement but that didn't stop her from going to Akwasi's house.

"Good to s-see you! How is m-my friend and how was it in A-Accra?"

"Everything went okay except for a fight with them the very first day."

"A-Again?"

"Yes, he was getting on my nerves. He thought I wasn't worth anything in his bed so he was going to spend all the time with you know who."

"Why did you c-come to see-see me so hurriedly? There m-must be something on y-your mind."

"Indeed yes. I have something to discuss with you."

"What?" he said and came to the table, cupped his hand under his chin and listened attentively.

"You know I am a victim of a bad marriage and . . . ."

"Yes, I do."

"And you also know how this terrible victimization has brought us closer together."

"I know but get to the point."

"I had thought of going to the powerful Agoro fetish to settle some scores with Agya Sei but I didn't want to let one woman's decision bring terror to her own husband. I have come to see you to get your approval lest I get swayed by my own natural goodheartedness."

"I f-for one think it's the l-last resort. I would do-do it if I-I were you."

Certainly, Akwasi knew exactly why he was saying this—a traitor.

"Thank you I lacked the courage to implement it but this is encouragement enough."

"Why do-don't you s-see Akua also for a helping s-suggestion."

"As for her she will go for it by all means. She hates his guts. I will go to her on Friday." It had rained heavily on Thursday night. Friday morning was cooler than other mornings so Abena took her bath with warm water. She wore her traditional cloth and also put on an old but decent looking sweater. She was off to Akua's place.

"Hello, how is it? I heard you went to dada," she said while looking for a glass to offer her mother water.

"Accra is a nice place but it is the same old story with your father."

"But it's you who let him do all that he does. You are too soft. If I were you I would seek help from some juju or voodoo man like a "kramo" or a fetish priest."

"You hit it right on the head of the nail. In fact, that's exactly why I am here, to seek your suggestion."

"Go ahead with it." Akua said forcefully because she had grown to loathe her father.

"I want you to go with me to this famous Agoro fetish."

"Why not, I will do that?"

Abena was resolved but not completely. The month's intervention that she thought of fulfilling her diabolical desire could probably change her mind. She smiled broadly to relieve herself of the doubt. Akua smiled back simultaneously nodding her head and telling her that it was the right thing to do.

Meanwhile in Accra, Agya Sei was looking for a good day to come to the village. He was resolute with a decision. He figured that he could take Friday off and come home for a long weekend.

At home in the village, he said to Abena,

"I have an important information to relate to you."

"That must be serious if you came all the way from Accra to tell me."

Agya Sei broke the news without beating about the bush.

"I must make it abundantly clear to you that I want my freedom."

"You mean you want a divorce?" She said calmly as if her husband's words didn't let her heart miss a beat.

"Yes, that's what I mean."

"Why this?"

"We don't get along, period."

"That's not good enough reason. I suspect something. In the past it would have been mean of you to say this to me. Is it Boatemaa? Tell me I will understand."

"No it's my own decision and I don't want you to implicate her."

"Well, if you are intently bent upon this decision, then I will let my relatives know about it immediately." She was shedding melancholy tears and let out a string of sobs and went outside leaving Agya Sei to sit and brood.

Two days after Agya Sei's disclosure, Akua heard of it. She, immediately, went to Kodie to ascertain the verity of it all. Abena confirmed it.

"I told you to do it and you were dilly-dallying."

"I will do it for a fact now," Abena said with confidence.

"Why don't we go today," Akua suggested.

"Sure."

While at the fetish shrine, the Priest asked them if they wanted to resolve the matter peaceably. Akua said no and urged Abena for a real jinx against her father. The fetish Priest demanded some important things including a bottle of schnapps, a white fowl and a dozen eggs. They went back and brought the stuff. They told the Priest exactly what should happen. He took the schnapps and went to the river god and appeased him with the gifts. The river god drink the liquor profusely. He invoked on its powers to let their requests, diabolical ones, come true. Abena and Akua came home with a light feeling of contentment as the onerous burden had been attended to and unloaded from their tired backs. As they waited for the anathema to take effect, the divorce was finalized, as Agya Sei was adamant to pleadings of his children.

Abena and Akua waited, for they believed in the Agoro fetish in toto. Those who had eyes beyond ordinary vision and ears to hear the imperceptible could discern prodigies from commonplace occurrences. Black Magic, Black Magic! Yes!

Meanwhile, at Accra, the first announcement for a wedding had already been given at the Holy Spirit Cathedral. Papa Adjei and his wife were already in town to help with the occasion. Akwasi, for the first time, had enough reason to turn down his friend's invitation. Finally, the appointed date for the wedding came. Agya Sei was resplendent in his tuxedo and Boatemaa looked like a saint in her white gown and veil. Nkwantabisa was a flower boy. Many dignitaries converged on the Holy Spirit Cathedral where the solemn service took place. The reception that followed was an elaborate one which words alone could not describe. There was no alleviation of Abena's grief when she found out about the wedding. She prayed for the true whole-hearted jinx against her former husband.

Much later in the year, as if by a foreboding omen, there appeared to be much dissension in the rank and file of the military. One early morning, the twelfth of the month to be exact, as sudden as a landslide, there was a broadcast on the Ghana Boradcasting Corporation radio.

"Fellow citizens of Ghana, today a prospective better government has been installed. Our poor country has been abused politically and worse of all, economically by the previous government. Their rule was corrupt and biased for the few. The people at the grassroots felt the bitterest pinge. We have come to liberate the country from the monster of economic mismanagement and mounting debt. We seek to bring peace and health after such a long malaise in the economic sector. We are tired of devaluations of our currency and the onerous burden they have on the average citizen. Our standard of living has been lowered to such an extent that we cannot bear it any longer. We anticipate a total support and cooperation from the oppressed masses. It is a new National Military Council—A revolutionary Council. This is Brigadier Rockson your new leader."

The change of government was too sudden to comprehend but yes, Black Magic, Mojo, juju and voodoo were at their working best. The jinx has been effected. Former members of government were asked to report to the nearest police station for their own safety until the inevitable williwaw subsided. There was no choice for Agya Sei. His heart jumped to his mouth upon awareness of the jolt to his government.

"Those rotten soldiers. What do they know about politics and democracy? Damn fools," he cursed. For the last time, he rode in the government Mercedes to the nearby police station. Over there, he received the first manhandling. One police man had pulled him so violently after he elicited stubborn arrogance that his head hit a gate rather too hard that he was bruised.

Boatemaa showed unusual boldness and calm in the absence of her husband. She persuaded the watchman to be faithful and vigilant to watch over the house. He complied.

Meanwhile, Abena was exultant. She quickly went to Akwasi's house.

"Have you heard the news?" Abena asked with an ear to ear smile.

"Yes, it is the-the c-coup-d'etat."

"These damn traitors are out for good. Agya Sei is going to smell pepper now. From grace to grass, he is going to be."

"They s-said the leader is B-Brigadier Rockson. He is a-a Fanti."

"Well, Fantis and Ashantis, same people."

Some soldiers and policemen, uneducated but wielding guns, found it necessary to abuse their new authority. Some were in the markets harassing traders. They contended that their prices were too exorbitantly priced. They maligned the sanctity and integrity of the new government. Later, some of the former government officials were released. These included Agya Sei.

Boatemaa saw her husband's face enveloped in much confusion. Realizing this she didn't bother him with unnecessary talk. She felt a wifely compassion for him as he came home and transformed into a silent mess. She was, however, able to convince Agya Sei to leave Accra for Kumasi immediately. She tried many unsuccessful attempts to appease him but he seemed to be characterized by lack of inclination or impetus to exertion.

"You shouldn't let things get to you so much. After-all, you've got me and Nkwantabisa."

Agya Sei wouldn't say anything but heave aggrieved sighs out of his confusion and suffering anguish.

Six months after the coup d'etat and their stay at Asokwa, tragedy hit again. Black magic, juju, mojo and voodoo, yes! Little Nkwantabisa had been playing with a small ball on the top floor without much vigilance from either the parents or grandparents. He had thrown the ball on to the eaves of the roof and sought desperately to retrieve it. In his child's mind, he thought he could get to it by climbing on top of the low railings around the fringes of the second floor. Unfortunately for him, he fell to critical injury of the back. Upon recognition of his whimpering sounds, Agya Sei rushed downstairs followed by Boatemaa. Without much delay, they took the car and sped to the emergency ward of the Okomfo Anokye Hospital. A doctor was summoned immediately. On arrival, he tried frantic efforts to bring life to the mortally injured and almost lifeless Nkwantabisa. He was almost successful in the initial stages, however, Nkwantabisa didn't recover and died a very precipitate death. The hastiness of it was quite obscene.

Uncontrollable tears and ululations broke down from Boatemaa. She just couldn't take the death phenomenon as it had robbed her of the very life she cherished most. Nkwantabisa was all her life. Her female ego was all epitomized in this son. She could never forgive herself for her lack of vigilance. She felt conscious of her guilt-ridden mind.

Church service followed a hasty traditional burial and funeral. Agya Sei remained silent all the time but actually he was in severe melancholia. He was depressed to the point of suicide. His sound psychological makeup was taken away first, by the coup d'etat which had robbed him of his grandiose and lavish livelihood and second, the death of the son he loved.

Agya Sei exhibited withdrawal in his daily routine and was characterized by insomnia at night. He also showed a definite sense of inadequacy and abnormal fatigability. Boatemaa sought the help of a medical doctor she knew and he confirmed that Agya Sei was suffering from some serious form of clinical depression, a form of mental illness.

"He'll need some institutionalization," the doctor told Boatemaa.

"Will he need to be taken to Ankaful Sanatorium in Cape Coast or Asylum in Accra?" she asked with grave concern.

"Yes, definitely. He needs some solitude for a quite recovery." Agya Sei was taken to Ankaful where recovery wasn't manifest until after a whole year. Boatemaa paid several visits to her demented husband but the duration of the intervals became longer and longer as the year progressed. Sometimes, his hopelessness was beyond question and he evoked sympathetic pity.

Meanwhile, Boatemaa began to have doubts about her husband's recovery. Her beautiful self had succeeded in enticing a young doctor friend. The only thing left to complete the illicit amour was the final seduction in his or her bed. Finally, they did it. Boatemaa couldn't hold back any longer. It was a Friday night after the doctor had treated her to an exceptionally lavish cuisine at the City Hotel plus a rather seductive "smooching" dance all night. When they got back to her premises she was totally surprised by his out-of-the-way aggressiveness. Much unlike Agya Sei, he seemed to be possessed by the devil and wanted a lot from her. He would groan and pant over and over. He was given to fierceness and unrestrained brutality in his love making. Despite all this, Boatemaa loved her friend's insatiability as contrasted with Agya Sei's lack of it. Her infidelity was quite natural she thought. She felt no guilt and said that circumstances had dictated the novel situation. Boatemaa had slowly become unsympathetic to Agya Sei's plight, quite forgetful of her marriage vow.

After much reconnoitering by the doctor, much to the disapproval of Papa Adjei and wife, he mustered enough courage and said to Boatemaa,

"Have you ever thought that you need a husband with more youthful vigor than this your demented old man?"

She glanced quickly at him and puzzled.

"No, the thought hasn't come to me yet. Why?"

"Have you ever thought of marrying again." She was surprised and said, "But you know I have a husband, why do you ask?"

"What! To an old-timer? I don't think he will ever regain sanity, and by the way, his complete mental integrity has been tarnished by this shameful bout."

"You are a doctor. You shouldn't say that of sick people."

"Disregarding his affliction now, he is too old for you. Now you don't have any entanglement with him after all Nkwantabisa is dead. His age coupled with his new condition will surely make him overly impotent. Now tell me how you would want to stay with an old, impotent and demented husband," as he said this he searched his lanky body for his cigarettes and matches. He placed one cigarette stick between his lips and lit a match. It went off. He lit another one and drew a long and voluminous inhalation. He puffed and filled the space between him and Boatemaa with jets of smoke. Boatemaa regarded his hazy features through the smoke. He looked feminine but he was by no means lacking in virility. His fair color, bushy hair, wide eyes, small lifted nose and an average mouth made him look like a mulatto. He was unique in his handsomeness and she couldn't imagine having seen any other face more appealing to look at. She said after a bit.

"I can appreciate what you are saying but note that it was he who made me the woman you see and lust after today."

"Of all the sophisticated women I have got to know, it's only you who wants to be attached to a madman."

"He is no longer mad when he is cured."

"Who said it can be cured, I am a doctor, it can only be treated. It can also be chronic. Do you want to live with that?" Boatemaa was coming back to her senses because she said,

"Our wedding vows said, "For better for worse, in happiness and in sickness."

"Forget about these meaningless white man's ideals. Even they, don't pay attention to their own beliefs. Don't you know that when they started coming to Africa it was the same ship which brought the Bible that also brought the bottles of whiskey and rum and took away slaves. What does the Bible say about strong drink?" He stood up and walked towards the fridge. "Divorce is most rampant in America where you travelled and cherish the people for their advancement. They are not so civilized when it comes to good and lasting marriages."

"What are you trying to get at with all these sermons all night?"

"I would like us to get married the traditional way, it's better. Don't worry about formal divorce with Agya Sei. He is sick and, be honest, won't you marry if he is perpetually crazed?"

"I will, of course, I am young."

"Well said, what's holding you?"

"Let me think about this for a while. I will give you an answer the same time next week."

Two days after the encounter with the doctor she still didn't know what to think. She took the car to Kodie to consult with friends about the idea of remarrying in keeping with the suggestions of the doctor.

"Are you passing over an offer by a real medical doctor to marry you, oh, oh," her long time friend said with some consternation.

"I haven't decided yet," Boatemaa said not necessarily surprised as her friend. She thought the general myth about medical doctors should be broken.

"I won't even give it a thought. I will accept it right away whether I was married or not," her friend said.

"What about if you were married to the Head of State. Come on be sensible," Boatemaa explained.

"Be realistic yourself. This husband you are trying to protect has had his glories gone by. He was once a somebody; now he is a nobody. You are even lucky to have someone with the caliber and social status of a doctor to ask you at all. Go for it."

Another friend said; "It's pathetic that our society views this sickness with the most grostesque debasement, it shouldn't be because we are all human and very susceptible to afflictions. You could be next you know. Sickness is no respector of persons."

"What should I do then, you think?" Boatemaa seemed confused indeed.

"I would wait a while until he is pronounced totally incapable of his marital responsibilities and there is enough evidence of no possible recuperation. Then you have every reason to go ahead and marry again."

Boatemaa thought this second friend's ideas were good but she refused to be convinced. Deep down, she had begun to have an aversion for Agya Sei by reason of his ailment and began clandestinely to love the doctor. She was in love and had become incredibly stupid by it. She saw the light quite clearly but she sought to obscure it with evasions and fantasies of her own imaginings. She dared to declare a positive answer to the doctor because she feared no rebuff, afterall, the whole precocious romance was his to begin with. Two days and nights passed by. She met the doctor again on Friday night. He again wined and dined her. While they were at it she disclosed her positive answer for marriage to him. He accepted it with complacency and designated the tenth of March for their traditional marriage. A few friends and relatives gathered on the tenth to witness the marriage of the doctor and Boatemaa illegally. She wore a multi-colored kente skirt and a light blue camisole. The doctor also were a kente cloth and a white jumper. Their traditional wedding was simple but the reception was elaborate. It was at the City Hotel again where they first met. They spent some time honeymooning at the hotel, after which they came back to Boatemaa's residence at Asokwa. Papa Adjei and wife said they had washed their hands off the new marriage of their daughter. They didn't particularly like the doctor because they thought he was an opportunist and just taking advantage of Boatemaa's good fortunes. Her house spoke for itself and the Mercedes she drove was nothing to joke about. Papa Adjei regarded the marriage with contemptuousness although Boatemaa was complacent and in high spirits. She was elated in the fact that she had met her match in all aspects.

Meanwhile, at Kodie, Akwasi had enthusiastically proposed to Abena who accepted with much appreciation and copious gratitude. Akwasi's father officiated a solemn marriage for them.

Abena entered the marriage with a sense of new elation. Now that Akwasi had taken control of her, life promised to be a bit easier and less burdensome. Akwasi, although not given to extravagance and obtrusive wealth, was a composed and rustic man with a touch of sincere human sensitivity. For a brief reception, Akua invited them to a delicious chicken and peanut soup and fufu. Instead of imbibing water to wash down the morsels, Akua bought Coca Cola as a treat to the wedded couple. She served crunchy biscuits for dessert, and was happy with those additions considering her meager resources. When the whole gang had finished eating the fufu, they slowly drank the soda and masticated the sweet biscuits with obliging contentment.

Akwasi, who was middle aged, had youthful vigor in his attitude towards romance. He took Abena, arm in arm, and strolled in a zesty way the narrow paths in the full moon. Abena was full of youthful exuberance herself and was genuinely pleased at the presence and complete captivity of Akwasi. They went back to village and their sleep was filled with pleasant dreams which they discussed and laughed about in the morning. What happy couple already!

CHAPTER 15

Agya Sei's children asked their brother, Kwaku, to go to Ankaful Sanatorium to visit him. He set out on the journey and at Oguaa or Cape Coast, he waited several minutes at Kotokoraba lorry station before he got the bus to Ankaful. While waiting, he ate one of the barbecued Akrantse (grasscutter) khebabs which were so ubiquitous and famous at Yamoransa Nkwanta. He bought them and some fruits for Agya Sei.

At Ankaful, a patient led him to his father. He was terribly psychotic, paranoid and worse of all he was having a bout of his asthma. He was totally alienated from what was real. He almost didn't recognize Kwaku.

"Dada it's me, Kwaku."

He took a long stare at his face and started a smile which later developed into a loud laugh.

"What's funny Dada? I am sorry I didn't come here earlier. It's because of school." Agya Sei laughed on. There must be some joy to madness which is only known to the madman because why should Agya Sei be laughing so hard at the visit of his son. Well, it was not all laughs because in a short time Agya Sei was sobbing uncontrollably. Gees, there must also be sorrow associated with madness. Kwaku also felt unshed tears in his eyes. To appease his father he brought out the Akrantse-on-a stick for his father. His eyes lit when he saw the four sticks. Kwaku was relieved. He ate heartily and speedily the bits of peppered meat. Obviously, he was enjoying it.

"How is the food here?"

"Not good at all," he strained to say and took short, wheezy breaths of sighs. Kwaku realizing his father's asthmatic condition asked,

"Have you seen the doctor?"

"No."

Kwaku didn't want to bother his father with more questions so he turned to the nurse to report his father's condition.

"Oh we have given him some shots. He will soon be better." She said with a lackadaisical air typical of some nurses who work with people but are not sensitive to the suffering of their patients. One particular nurse though, was very concerned about Agya Sei and used to tell him stories to cheer him up. Agya Sei appreciated her wholeheartedly. She was instrumental in bringing Agya Sei out of delusions and hallucinations. She alone anticipated anxiously the best possible recuperation for Agya Sei. Kwaku stayed with the father for quite a while and later asked to go.

"Be here often because visits of this sort cheer patients up a lot and help them get better," said the nurse.

"Alright."

Fortunately for him, after this visit, he was getting better and better. Ignorant of the things that had come to pass in his absence and sojourn into derangement, Agya Sei, upon getting better, girded himself for a sole romantic reawakening with Boatemaa because as usual thoughts of her were his standard hope and perhaps helped in his recuperation. This was so despite the fact that Boatemaa had just about stopped visiting him completely, as she considered him hopelessly deteriorated into the realms of eccentricity. When he started getting better he would ask begging questions to everybody around him as to the gracefulness of Boatemaa. Those who had seen her during her initial visits agreed with him vehemently. They alluded to her marked sophistication and this whipped up his spirits into a better gear. The irrepressible and haunting

127

thoughts about why Boatemaa had stopped visiting didn't put a dent on his escalated spirits. He just couldn't wait to see his wife.

Before long he was completely out of his mental cocoon at Ankaful and was at Asokwa noticeably perked up by honest, good thoughts about Boatemaa. She was the only one at home. With unwarranted fear of Agya Sei's presence and unable to ponder at his recovery, she stammered and said,

"Wha-what brings you here?"

"Don't be silly I am well. The hospital helped me to come. Let's rejoice."

Boatemaa's stare was not focused. Her heart started pounding. She was looking at him in the eye but her thoughts were a millennium apart. She brought herself back to her senses and said,

"You are well?"

"Yes, of course, can't you tell. I am a different person now."

Boatemaa's recent problem was enormous. A cold chill swept through her spine. The doctor, the doctor, my new husband, my new husband! She had for a moment forgotten herself and Agya Sei had to constantly remind her of what to do.

"Won't you give me something to drink? I could also use something to eat. I am famished." Boatemaa hurried to the refrigerator and got a bottle of ice water and poured Agya Sei a fill. He could notice her trembling hands.

"What is the matter?"

"Nothing."

Agya Sei couldn't understand his wife's constant introspection so he pulled a chair and sat her down.

"What's the problem?"

"I am no longer good for you, isn't it. He was full of self pity."

"That's not the case. I am just not well and moreover I wasn't expecting you."

"Oh, you thought I wouldn't get better. Is that right?"

"I am not thinking about your ailment."

"What are you thinking of then?" He asked much puzzled by his wife's evasiveness.

"Nothing," she said again.

In the meantime, the doctor had finished a hectic day at the hospital and was returning with a wearied mind and soul to the welcoming and comforting arms of Boatemaa. He drove her Mercedes possessively. He was stultifying, and unmindful of imminent strife. The superb comfort of the car was enough for him to indulge in breaking traffic regulations. He delighted in overspeeding past slower cars in front of him and wherever he observed the road ahead without any potholes he would zoom in a surge. In his unrestrained pleasure at speeding he was home in fifteen minutes. He entered the garage and honked the horn.

"Who is that?" Agya Sei asked sharply. Boatemaa rushed to the door. The doctor was right there. His usual carefree attitude sped him past Boatemaa to Agya Sei.

"What is he doing here?" the doctor asked. Boatemaa remained silent as a dumb person. After the two men regarded each other for an awkward half minute, Agya Sei stood and went to Boatemaa,

"What is this young man doing in the house?" He turned immediately towards the doctor and said,

"Get out of here."

"It's you who should get out, you are intruding."

Boatemaa still stood dumbfounded. Just in the nick of time, Papa Adjei and wife entered the room. They saw the obvious bad situation and instinctively came to their daughter's rescue.

"Hello Agya Sei, how are you?" Papa Adjei said.

"Don't you hello me, hypocrites. All of you get out of this house and I said immediately."

"This is not your house, it's legally mine," Boatemaa said.

"Are you nuts?"

"You were. You were my husband, you aren't any longer. I am married again to this man.", pointing to the doctor.

"Who gave you the go ahead?"

"Your belated sickness did."

"Is that so?"

"Yes, that's so."

Agya Sei furious as well as confused, saw that there were four people against him in the room. Definitely, somebody must go out to ease the tension. Agya Sei saw himself to be the one so he took his bag, gave Boatemaa a deep and severe look, and walked past the three towards the door numbed by morbid anger.

Already aware of his precarious psychological state, he controlled himself and his thoughts. The last thought that came to him was to go to nearby Asokwa police station to make a case out of the awkward state of affairs. His report was brief. He said a trespassing, young intruder had come to kick him out of his own house. The sergeant recognized Agya Sei and called the attention of his superintendent. Without dilly-dallying, the superintendent himself accompanied by two constables took the jeep and went to the house.

Boatemaa was surprised to find the policemen in her house. Her parents were all of a sudden trembling, the doctor was nonchalant and Agya Sei felt a triumphant relief. After a brief investigation, the superintendent ordered the doctor to leave or face violent ejection. He tried some arrogance but he was thrown out of the house before he could say anything. The two constables were left behind to keep peace until such a time that there was no more trouble from the doctor.

Papa Adjei, his wife and Boatemaa were all obviously in a very embarrassing state. How could they convince Agya Sei of their daughter's impropriety at marrying the doctor and last of all her sinister action towards her husband when he arrived from the hospital. Papa Adjei was profuse in his apologies. He even out of humility and mendicity knelt on his one good knee in front of Agya Sei to show how he seriously thought about the whole situation.

Boatemaa realized, after the doctor was gone, her mistake and uselessness in defending their illicit marriage. She cupped her hands in constant pleas for mercy. Boatemaa's mother joined in too. Agya Sei couldn't bear the sight of his once loved relations in abhorrent mendicancy. He yielded to their pleas and warned that he wouldn't tolerate any more bad behavior especially from Boatemaa. The silence that evening was charged and was even heightened by the surveillance of the constables outside the house and Agya Sei's utter incredulity at his wife's behavior.

The doctor hadn't learned any lesson from this encounter. He still paid secret visits to Boatemaa and insisted that their common law marriage was right. He tried many times to persuade her to extricate herself from the loose grips of this old man whose mental capacity was vulnerable to emotional injury. Boatemaa had almost consented to his pleas but for the timely discussion one morning with the father while Agya Sei was out.

"Tell him off. You need to become one with Agya Sei again."

"How?"

"If you are incapable of this I will help you."

What Papa Adjei wasn't aware of was the deep feeling of affection of hers for the doctor. For some reason, she couldn't bring herself to accept the fact of her love for the doctor and the now discernable abomination of Agya Sei. She sought to resolve the ominous conflict.

Meanwhile, the constables whom the doctor bribed lavishly were also clandestine liaisons to Agya Sei. He was well aware of the goings on and was planning something to avenge his soured heart.

One early Saturday morning, Agya Sei informed Boatemaa that he was going to Kodie. His plans were two-fold. He would seek the help of some young stalwart friends at the village to help him teach the doctor a lesson. He planned to go back to Asokwa with the "wild" young men in the evening for he could tell of the doctor's presence at the house with much discriminating accuracy.

Sure enough, the doctor had received information through one of the policemen that Agya Sei had gone away in the morning and won't be back till the next morning. The doctor, as foolhardy as he was, came and spent almost the whole day in the house. Boatemaa shouldn't have entertained him but surprisingly and foolishly she was happy with him around. It looked as if the doctor had made some strong juju or voodoo on her which kept her under his spell.

As night drew close with its somber and sinister darkness, Agya Sei hired taxi cabs filled with his youngster thugs. They were roused to combativeness and aggression by Agya Sei's insistence that they carry sticks and anything that could inflict severe punishment on a man. They were wild with fury and talked about evil thoughts filled with elements of brutality. Of course, Agya Sei had bought them plenty of akpeteshie.

Agya Sei and the six stalwart young men arrived at a time when the policemen were dozing. Immediately, three of the lads took care of them. Just then, the doctor came out followed by Boatemaa. One lad, evidently the strongest, accosted him by saying,

"What do you think you are doing in this house?" He roughed the doctor with a tight and strong pull at his shirt. He was slightly off his feet.

"Police," the doctor shouted. To his surprise, there was no word from them. He tried to break free but another strong lad joined in his manhandling. There was genuine shock and astonishment in his expression. After a brief scuffle, he was bundled off his feet and carried into the waiting taxi cab. They sped away to an undisclosed destination. Meanwhile, Boatemaa had broken into tears, sobbing copiously at the rumpus.

"Where are they taking him?" she asked.

A sharp slap exhibited Agya Sei's resentment. This time he was really angry with her. He pulled her violently inside.

"Let go off me," she tried to wring her hand free. Agya Sei held tighter and pushed her into one of the couches in front of him. As Papa Adjei and wife were out, there was no one to come to her aid and she felt some timorousness. Agya Sei felt extreme malice in him. He pounded Boatemaa with a couple of strong jabs and left her to cry on the sofa. Boatemaa's mother, as if predestined, came out of nowhere and saw her daughter in a slumped mess.

"What is it again?"

Agya Sei was too choleric to talk. She helped Boatemaa up and out.

The five men were merciless in the beatings they gave to the doctor. He had been knocked unconscious with blood oozing from his mouth and nose. One tooth was loose and he lay in complete torpor along the dirt road, made bushy and desolate by very tall elephant grasses. He did not know where he was and was in terrible pain. After he painstakingly crawled to the lone tree on the left side of the road he saw a faint glimmer of light. Afterwards he heard the sound of the oncoming vehicle and knew at once that it was a motor cycle. It sped right past him without stopping. Fortunately, what sounded like a car came along and stopped. In the car was an older man and a young girl.

What they had come to do in so desolate a place was enough to make one wonder. The driver got down and saw the doctor.

"What is he doing here?" the young girl asked.

"He looks severely beaten, can't you see?"

"He must be a thief then," the girl said.

An agonized "no" came from the pained lips of the doctor.

"If you're not a thief, what are you?" He tried to speak but only a low indistinct and incoherent sound came out. The young girl was able to convince the man that the mortally hurt doctor was a thief and thus shouldn't be helped. The man agreed and left him despite his incessant murmurings of protest. He lay there till the crack of dawn. He couldn't sleep and lay awake in the cool night in fearful torment. A little bit of his lottery state left him as he walked with considerable effort into the empty road ahead of him.

Finally a car approached. The driver stopped to see the situation and knew right away that the doctor was hurt. The driver took him to the Okomfe Anokye Hospital and visited him all the time he was in the hospital.

After he got better, the doctor did not rest his case notwithstanding the fact that he couldn't trace the thugs. But, of course, he remembered that it was Agya Sei who brought them that fateful night. He decided to press charges against Agya Sei. The Superintendent at the Central Police Station whom the doctor had bribed lavishly took the charges very seriously. The case was taken to court and the six thugs were rounded up and arrested through the help of Agya Sei.

After long court proceedings, the judge upon recommendation from the jury, announced his verdict in the packed court. He gave three years of hard labor to each of the six men for aggravated assault and intent to murder. Agya Sei got a year for conspiracy to intentionally eliminate the doctor.

After some time in prison, Agya Sei was finding life very detestable and utterly debasing. He elicited return to psychological disintegration and his depression was acute. He was peevish, pessimistic and suffered gravely from insomnia. His new situation at the prison had gone unnoticed while his mind was full of thoughts with extreme suicidal tendencies. He often made jejune remarks on the conditions and treatment at the prison. Sometimes, his bewilderment was beyond his own routine control. One night, after he had stayed awake for nearly five hours his suicidal tendencies returned. With teeth and hands he tore his bed covers into long strands and improvised a taut rope with a noose. Somehow he got the rope around one of the high bars and the noose around his neck and jumped a fatal jump to a very, very unfortunate and very, very sad successful suicide.

After his death and funeral, Abena thought the black magic juju had gone too far. She felt some sadness but soon it was forgotten.

Somehow Boatemaa and the doctor got back again and perhaps they felt no guilt and were happy.

AFRICAN CELEBRATION

BY

STEPHEN KWAME MENDS

These messages are meant to challenge the minds of Africans, African-Americans and whites alike. They incorporate African cultural beliefs, history, and religion as seen by the author.

AFRICAN RAINY SEASON

Let the first warm rains of the season wash away
our tears and let contentment fill our hearts once again.

The drought was long but it is gone
The animals are back from their long migration.

If the zebra had tears it will weep no more
If the giraffe had tears it will weep no more
If the silverback had tears it will weep no more
And even if the lion had tears, it will weep no more.

For the new rains are life in full
It is renaissance
It is abundance.

Let the anxious farmers clutch their hoes and cutlasses.

Oh heavy falling rains, pelt our aluminum roofs and
make a racket as you did a long time ago
Fall down into little running streams
Let gutters overflow their banks
And let puddles be ever omnipresent.

New life of first rains
Renew our lives, for, the downs are no more
And the ups are coming.

AN AFRICAN'S SURPRISE—SEPTEMBER 11, 2001

In July 1971, I had journeyed to New York, my first time
indeed and seen the imposingly majestic World Trade
Centers' mesmerizing architectural feats and ingenuity.
Yet, on September 11, 2001, as I sat in my plush living
room in Rhode Island watching television at 9 a.m., I
saw dark smoke billowing from the left tower. Five
minutes later I saw a plane chisel through the right
tower like a hot knife cutting through a stick of butter.

A huge conflagration erupted. Was I watching a movie
or was it real? Who had defied all American sophisticated
technology and intelligence to cause this devastating
tragedy?

Later, I saw both towers crumble down in an enraged
display of huge black and white smoke and dust. People
ran helter-skelter. It was suggested the Arabs did it.
Osama bin Ladin's name flashed, then Mohammed Atta's, etc.

Are the Muslims so envious of America that they are becoming
the barbarians of the Roman Empire? No! America
is still strong; united under President George W. Bush.
Those Muslims must be brought to justice and terrorists
defeated!

God bless America. But be careful, we have a new enemy.

P.S.

In 2011, almost ten years after that awful and never-to-be-forgotten day, our new, first great black president, Barack Obama, in a television broadcast, announces to America that the demon architect of many innocent deaths had been killed himself. "Osama bin Ladin is dead."

Thank you Barack Obama; thank you Goerge W. Bush; thank you Dick Cheney. Long Live America!

AFRICAN HISTORY

Memory is a bane to those who have seen misfortune before
Mother Africa, forget your slavery.
Mother Africa, forget your colonialism.
Mother Africa, forget the unjust economic world order.
Mother Africa, even forget the former Apartheid.
Really, how can you?
Mother Africa, still forget the plunder and pillage;
Forget the technological stagnation and be content.
For you are the only one with unadulterated Black people
You are the only one with authentic flora and fauna.
You are the only one with unpolluted air
You are the only one without hazardous nuclear radioactive waste
You are still the only one with virgin rainforests.
Let them destroy their environment in the name of advancement
Be content, for I am singing a lullaby all for you.
Yes, don't worry, you'll sleep someday and have the last laugh.

AN AFRICAN'S FIRST WINTER

Oh beautiful white snowflake!

Are you

Just from the sky?

Or

Indeed you are from heaven!

Join

Your friends and fall to the ground

Into a

Pristine carpet of immaculate whiteness.

Does it snow in heaven?

It must be, for your cold, soft, white riot

Is like

God's own soul, pure, untainted, and holy,

Oh beautiful snowflake, show us God.

AN AFRICAN'S GOOD MORNING

Oh blessed me!

I am like the lark.

Unlike the owl,

I will sleep early and wake up early.

To sing and praise God,

And breathe

His fresh morning air.

And see his beautiful sunrise.

Oh beautiful creation,

Make humans

Like larks

So, they'll praise you unconditionally.

AFRICAN COLOR CONCEPT

Alas!, black is not beautiful according to white interpretation
Afterall, just take a look at "BLACK" the ugly in the English dictionary
BLACK ART
BLACK AFRICA
BLACK BOOK
BLACK LIST
BLACK FACE
BLACK FLAG
BLACK GUARD
BLACK HEAD
BLACK HOLE
BLACK LEG
BLACKMAIL
BLACK SHEEP
ETC ETC ETC
all black and evil.
Then take a look at "WHITE" the beautiful.
WHITE HOUSE
WHITE HEAD
WHITE SNOW
WHITE COLLAR
WHITE ELEPHANT
WHITE CAP
WHITE BOOK
WHITE CHRISTMAS
WHITE HEADED
WHITE PERSON
No wonder the white man calls us black.

AFRICAN RELIGION

OUR GODS ARE STILL ALIVE BUT
WHITE MAN'S GOD IS JEALOUS BECAUSE HE SAYS

"I AM YOUR LORD THY GOD,
THOU SHALT NOT HAVE ANY OTHER GODS."

DON'T WE TOO HAVE A SUPERNATURAL?
SO THAT OUR IMPOSED GOD BE ONLY WHITE?

THE AFRICANS ARE THE ONLY PEOPLE WHO LEFT
THEIR GODS TO FOLLOW THE JEALOUS GOD TO BE
CIVILIZED

OUR GOD IS BLACK.
OUR GODS ARE BLACK.

TIGARE IS STRONG,
KWAKU FIRI IS ALSO STRONG,

AKONEDI IS STRONG,
ANTOA NYAMAA IS ALSO STRONG,

KANKAN NYAME IS STRONG,
KYERAMANG IS STRONG.
AGBALAGBA IS ALSO STRONG.

COME BACK OUR BLACK GOD.
COME BACK ONYANKOPON.
COME BACK CHUKWU.

FOR THE ONE WHO BROUGHT US THE GOOD AND
JEALOUS GOD,
SLAPPED US IN THE FACE AND TOOK US SLAVES FOR 400
YEARS

WHERE WERE YOU?

THEY STILL DISCRIMINATE
AGAINST US IN RACISM
IN LOW COMMODITY PRICES AND DEV ALUATIONS

IN PAINFUL STRUCTURAL ADJUSTMENTS,
AND IN WICKED DEBT BURDENS.

COME BACK NANA NYAME.
COME BACK AMADIORA
COME BACK IFEJIOKU
COME BACK OGUN

ALLAH IS STILL THERE
HARE KRISHNA IS THERE
CONFUCIUS IS STILL THERE
TAOISM IS STILL THERE

WHY OH, WHY WHITE MAN?

WHAT HAVE AFRICANS DONE?

"WELL, YOU ARE "NIGGERS," THIEVES AND GOD FORSAKING "COONS"

COME AND SHINE MY SHOES."

AN AFRICA ADVICE

At the height of civilization,

Please go back.

You climbed to the top of the ladder.

But

Don't ever forget your first step.

You flew a thousand miles.

But

Don't forget your first mile.

You counted with a calculator and a computer.

But

Don't forget to count again with your fingers or the abacus.

You have seen many religions.

But

Don't forget your Judaism.

You built magnificent cities, Babylon, Athens, Rome, New York, e.t.c.

But

Don't forget the cavemen, Eden or Jerusalem.

You grew to be a wise man or a woman.

But

Don't forget your infancy and childhood.

Now you run.

But

Always know you crawled first.

Be primitive again, go back to the basics.

And

Start running, building, climbing and always learning again.

AFRICAN BEAUTY

Not the fat
Not the double chin
Not the bulging belly
Not the fat butt
Not the Nkabankaba neck (neck with fatted rings)
Not the Crow's feet, wrinkles, or the turkey neck but

The subtle slim
The sublime slender
And the buxom belle

Beauty personified
Elizabeth Toro
Beauty personified
Dzidzo
Beauty personified
Irene
Beauty personified
Sarah,

Take shape and
Be dondo shaped (Dondo: Hourglass shaped or guitar shaped)
Be not a glutton
'cos
Fat is hypertension
Fat is stroke
Fat is sickness and laziness

Exercise?

Yes

Shape up and have a figure

AFRICAN Women!

AFRICAN DRUG PROBLEM

Cigarettes will give you cancer.
Yet you still make and smoke them.

Marijuana will make you psychotic.
Yet, you still want it.

L.S.D. and Heroin will make you hallucinate, delusional
Addicted and give you Aids.
Yet, you still want them.

Cocaine will kill you.
Yet, you still want it.

Pleasure SEEKERS and Foolish Hedonists
Are you just dumb or too CIVILIZED?

Well, COLOMBIA and Mexico SUPPLY THEM!
The best drug is the word of God.
It will make and take you very high
Even higher to heaven.

THE AFRICAN ARMY

The African Army is a haven of non-combatants
Where is your pugnacity?
Who will liberate Africa for us
If not through your bayonets nor
Your assegais, spears, poisoned arrows.
Don't be a complacent soldier bent on
Coup-making and quest for political power for
You are a soldier and you must be pugnacious
Don't we have an African war to win—yes
It is against Western F2 and F16 bombers and drones
It is against the vestiges of Colonialism
Pluck up your pugnacious courage
African soldier, for
Your life is one of futility, this is your choice
And inevitable death that comes sooner than . . . be
Dedicated and ready to die anytime for whom? For
Your continent, your country, your fellow civilians, for
You have chosen the path of ready death
Armez, Armez, Armez
Formez Vos Bataillons
et
Attaquez, Attaquez, Attaquez.

AN AFRICAN'S MARRIAGE

Oh divine mercy!
Just like Samson;
You gave me strength
To kill a lion with a spear,
Before you gave me my wife.
Good Lord, give me this same strength,
To love and marry till we die.
It's Valentine's Day today
And she looks as beautiful
As the day she was presented to me
In my thatched hut.
And that night was beautiful.

AFRICAN SEX

I am sexually mature by 15 but I am not
          ready for marriage yet
I can give birth at 13 but I am not ready
          to marry yet.
What can I do with all this pent up potential
          sex energy?
Ah! masturbate and don't feel guilty
          'cos, LORD,!
Masturbation without guilt is far, far
          better than
FORNICATION, ADULTERY, RAPE, MOLESTATION,
TEENAGE PREGNANCY, STDs AND AIDS.

AFRICAN SUNRISE AND SUNSET

Oh, African sun!
You are always so punctual.

By the time you come every morning
The Muezzin has called the faithful to prayer.

By the time you are in your regal majesty,
Some Catholics have already prayed.

You shine so bright that
Daylight is real daylight.

How I wish I was in Alexandria, Minnesota
So that I could see you rise on

Beautiful Lake Darling, and on
Charming Lake Cowdry

But your breathtaking sunset,
Is an eyes' delight.

Wake up African!
And see your GIFT
          in
Its full and splendid majesty.
Oh African Sun!

AFRICAN COOL MORNING AIR

AIR FOR SALE?
HA, HA, HA!
DO SOME PEOPLE REALLY SELL AIR?
YES!
U.S.A. HAS POLLUTED AIR
GREAT BRITAIN HAS POLLUTED AIR
WEST GERMANY HAS POLLUTED AIR
JAPAN HAS POLLUTED AIR
AND THEY SELL AIR IN THE FORM OF OXYGEN
AND IF HUMANS HAD ANY DIVINE POWER, MOST PEOPLE
WILL DIE
BECAUSE THEY WILL SELL AIR TO THE LESS FORTUNATE
AFRICA,
YOUR MORNING AIR IS SO
PURE, SO FRESH, SO COOL.
FILL MY LUNGS IN FULL VOLUME
COOL MY SKIN WITH ABUNDANT
LAPS
    YES
AFRICAN AIR YOU ARE
      SO COOL!

    AFRICAN STUPIDITY

Why this secondhand FUR COAT
In 100°F weather?
"I want to look like the white man"

156

Why this secondhand winter jacket and stocking cap
In this blazing December afternoon?
"Well white man wears it,
I swear, I have seen it in the video"
Why, oh why, black man are
You such a stupid copycat?
I think we still look better in
Our LOIN CLOTH.
      ANY COMMENT?

AFRICA THE BEAUTIFUL

We are proud and lucky to live in Africa
Where else can you get such sunshine?
Where else can you get such diverse wildlife
Where else can you watch a cheetah at top speed?

Be proud to be an African
We are poor, so what?
Hasn't any poor African outlived
The prosperous and well-cared for Caucasian,
And the luxurious Japanese?

Anyway, Brother African,
What is the most beautiful symmetrical
Map on the ATLAS?
AFRICA OF COURSE!
Does that click?
How happy I am to be an African!

AFRICAN INIQUITY?

Sodom and Gomorrah?
    Ask the Bible.

Sexual orgy?
    Ask drunken Lot.

Homosexuality and lesbianism?
    Ask Juvenal or Sappho.

PORNOGRAPHY, (Oh Calcutta, Deep Throat) etc.?
    Ask a Yankee or a Swede
    Or the Westerner
    AIDS?

Still ask a Yankee
    Oh Africa!
Why did we?
Why did we allow these Bible brandishing
Slavers on our shores.
They had the gun, and still have it,
they will kill to dominate.
They don't care, they will kill.
But did they create the human being
to kill him whether in war or whatever.
Only sin and God must kill.

AFRICAN ATHLETE

Strong force we are
The Marathon winners!

Strong force we are
The middle distance winners!

Strong force we are
We don't cheat in anabolic steroids.
We don't cheat in creatine,

Though poor we are,
We still run like the Cheetah

Tribute, Bikila Abebe
Tribute, Kipchonge Keino

Tribute, Said Aouita
Tribute, Abdi Bile

We don't cheat in steroids. Shame on you!

THE AFRICAN ATHLETE?

Yes, a proud and definitely honest mighty force.
We are hungry compared to you
But see us at the next Boston Marathon
And watch a very, very hungry African win it again. Ha!

AFRICAN SMILE AND LAUGH

DON'T BARE YOUR WHITE FALSE TEETH AT ME
IN
A FAKE, SUPERFICIAL SMILE,
BE
LIKE AN AFRICAN AND, LAUGH FROM YOUR
GUT
INTO A VERY HONEST AND HAPPY MIRTH
YES
INNOCENT AFRICAN SMILE,
THAT'S IT!

AFRICAN THANKS

If you read all this
and
Understand it
Go
Go
And thank your teachers immediately
White Master
We
Are indebted to you, really?

AFRICAN RESOURCE EXPLOITATION

GOLD,
DIAMOND,
IVORY,
ALL OURS.

URANIUM,
COPPER,
CHROME,
ALL OURS.

COCOA,
COFFEE,
PEANUTS,
ALL OURS.

MAHOGANY,
EBONY,
SAPELE,
ALL OURS.

OIL,
PHOSPHATE,
BAUXITE,
ALL OURS.

BUT WHO IS TAKING THEM?
ARE WE OR THEY ARE
AFRICA (GHANA) '83

Historical time in Africa
Historical time in Ghana
     DROUGHT
     BUSHFIRES
     FAMINE
     EMACIATION
     RAWLINGS' CHAIN
I had travelled from the United States,
The land of plenty
The land of grain stockpiles
The land of very many overweight and obese people
     to
GHANA (AFRICA)
     And what did I see?

The drought, famine and starvation
Had made our women
     SLIM
     SLENDER
     VERY BEAUTIFUL to the envy of the obese on diet.
We eat the little we have to live,
You live to eat the abundance you have to grow fat and not share
You have made us flex our overworked sinewy muscles to be
Hewers of wood and drawers of water for pittance
All you can do now is go on the BIGGEST LOSER
Who is sick now? You tell me!

AFRICAN DIET

Quaker Oats, milk and sugar?
Why not Akasa and Honey!

Cake, strawberry short cake, and Apple pie,
What about Apitsi, Abodo or tatar,
      Potatoes?
Why not plantain with the blessed iron?
      Apple?
What about Mango, Avocado Pear, Pineapple or
      Guava.
Coca Cola with caffeine?
Why not ice cold Elewonyo.

Sardines with carcinogenic preservatives?
What about mouth watering Ntsitsii.

Mad cow corned beef?
Why not Akrantse, Otwe or even Kyinkyinga?

Allow not colonialism to
Kill you.

Be African
Eat African and

Be an octogenarian
Or live a whole century

      Ebei!

AFRICAN PREDICAMENT

I am growing hairs on my teeth
Only me and who else?
      Why me, Lord?

My only genetic makeup
My only fate
My only destiny.

Solve my inherent problem for me
      Lord
              for
My famous hair gets in the
Way of my chewing stick and toothbrush.

AFRICAN LOVE

Sweet African love
Engulf us
                    for
You are like the "atadwe" (tigernut).
                    or the
Ripe mango
You are very sweet when
                    eaten
In the morning
You are very sweet when
                    eaten
In the afternoon,

You are also very sweet when
                    eaten
In the evening . . .
Sweet African love
                    be
In our lives always!

GOD'S VIDEO CAMERA

The sun
The moon
The myriad stars;
God's video cameras
Taking pictures
By day and night.
Righteousness?
Yes!
'Cos
On judgment day
Your
Video cassette will be shown
And
We'll all be your jury and your Judge.
God is not an autocrat!

AFRICAN ELEGY

Oh Africa,
Must the white man always enslave us?

Must the Chinese
Insult us?

Must Rudyard Kipling
Berate us?

Are we really God's Anathema?

Why, Oh Ham
Did you take a peek
At drunken naked Noah?

AFRICAN PLEA

Brother Nigger
Brother Negro
Brother Coloured Person
Brother Black American
Brother Afro American
Whatever they'll call you!

Finally, Brother African American
      (about time!)
Now I call you Diasporan African

Your roots are here in Africa
You can't deny it 'cos you're Black
Come to help Africa develop
'Cos you built America with your unpaid sweat

Look at Solidarity!
He went to South Africa and developed it.
     and
It's a battle wrestling it from him.
He went to the Falkland Islands,
Just to defend his color.

Where is Black Solidarity
Come back home Brother,
We'll welcome you
Come back home Sister
We'll welcome you.

Thanks to the White man
You forgot your culture and language
        but
All the languages are still here.
        and why, oh why
Haven't you come
        to
Learn Hausa,
        to
Learn Fanti
to
Learn Twi
        to
Learn Yoruba

I have learned
        English
        French
        Greek
        Latin
        Spanish
        Hebrew
But
Lord, I like black languages
        Fanti and Ashanti better
But alas, imperialism has not allowed me to learn to write them
Come back home honorable, sophisticated
A F R I C A N.

AFRICAN MALARIA

Just a bloody meal
   and
You are moribund.

You are so fragile
   and
Need only a slight tap

Yet so strong
You are our scourge.

Envious of humanity
You have anopheletic power
Defenseless we bring our Quines
Don't resist them, Plasmodium!

Weakness in your creation
Also power in your creation

Though you easily die
Your chills are unbearable

Thanks to you
The Colonialist found his grave

Without you I wonder
The intensity of our exploitation

But Anopheles, Culex!
Take pity now,

On this child!
African thanks.

AFRICAN FAITH

Only those who believe they can win
      will always win
Despite odds, I know for a fact that
Someday, with the succor of God,
We too will win, and then
Africa would have won all
Her battles.
      Really?

AFRICAN FEMALE VISAGE

Bleach the face,
Be near—white and be like Michael Jackson

Bleach the face
Get skin cancer.

Bleach the face
Get "Nanso Eben"

Black is beautiful!
Ebony is beautiful!

Did you see the diamond twinkling eyes
All set in black?

Did you see the pearly sparkling teeth
All set in black gums, so beautiful!

Did you see a white person wanting
To be Black?

Yet he will make Mercuric iodide
Yet he will mock us in minstrel show counterfeit
Black face with stereotypic buffoonery

Liberate yourself from neo-colonialism and
Enjoy being Black.

AFRICAN WOMAN!

AFRICAN LAZINESS

Don't we have a grain belt?
When will our bumper crop finally come?

Must we perpetually panhandle,
When the fertile fields beg of cultivation?

When solar energy is an African gift?
When abundant precipitation is also an African gift?

Where is our irrigation?
Look at Ethiopia.

Look at Sudan,
Look at Somalia,

We are our own responsibility.
Independence must be thorough.

The proud lion won't panhandle,
The swift cheetah won't panhandle,

The elegant giraffe won't panhandle,
Even though there is a drought.

AFRICA'S LAZINESS

He who does nothing will come to nothing
C'mon African leader, rule hard and well without being corrupt
African fisherman, work hard
African farmer, the hoe, the cutlass, grip them.
African teacher, c'mon you're intelligent, teach!
African doctor, we trained you, why exile yourself?
African policeman, why be corrupt!

C'mon African laborer, work hard.
Let's all get sweat on our brow
      to
Develop Mother Africa in our own way
Thus said Franz Fanon
C'mon African ingenuity, we have it, yes!
      Assert yourself!

AFRICAN LAZINESS

Some Africans are somehow lazy, however,
They are also good hard workers.
If you don't force the African
Lord, he might sleep the whole day,
                    but,
If you get him to work,
He'll work like a slave
America knows it.
I am not lying!

AFRICAN WAR CONCEPT

You say we are black savages
You say we are cannibals
You say we like too much fighting in
      STUPID TRIBAL WARS.

Lord knows you are civilized.
You also like too much fighting
Well, of course, in important
Well orchestrated, human decimating
      SAVAGE WORLD WARS.

Are you such a pessimist?
Are you so ANTI-MANKIND?

We are awaiting another major conflagration
Yes, we wait anxiously for
      BRUTAL THIRD WORLD WAR

Will it be Armageddon?
      then
God save the Queen first
      before
We all get wiped out, period!

AN AFRICAN'S NOSTALGIA

Today, I watched the breath-taking sunset
    In the west as usual
      and
Saw the brilliantly lit horizon for a spell
    Then I asked,
"What is beyond this serene horizon?"
Atlantic Ocean, of course!
No, even beyond that?
Then American, of course.
Ah yes, but where specifically?
I am thinking of Alexandria, Minnesota,
    Good!
Alex, is it the usual American Rat-Race?
    Or
It is still the love, the friendship, the smiles
The genuine altruism, the good laugh,
The kidding about winter and snow?

Oh Jefferson, my academic cocoon for a year!
Big Ole, are you still guarding Alex?
Is there anyone still skeptical about the Runestone?

Olson Supermarket, I miss your cauliflower,
Asparagus, cucumbers and zucchini.

It is almost 40 years ago since I first stepped on
Your tranquil fertile land, tranquil crystal

Clear lakes, tranquil rustic but merry people.

When shall we meet again?
Should it be till kingdom come?
or next year, next month, next week, or even tomorrow?
I miss you Alex.

> By Kwame Mends
> AFS son of Mr. & Mrs. Erc Aga and
> Mr. and Mrs. Walt Salt. (1971-1972)

ALEX, MINNESOTA THE BEAUTIFUL

Alexandria, my happy sojourn.

The glaciers did you so well

   'cos

Now you have majestic Lake Darling.

Now you have charming Lake Cowdry.

   'cos

Your walleyes,

Your northern pikes, your sunfish, your trout

Even your minnows,

   are

Mouth watering delights

For nature's other living things,

Look at that breathtaking sunrise

on Lake Cowdry

Look at that sensational sunset

on Lake Darling

Go to Alexandria for a

Truly, true, restful sojourn.

Solitude and comtemplative meditation

You'll enjoy everything.

MINNESOTA STATE BIRD

Why, oh why, Mr. Loon!
Why this strange SOS cry?
Are you lonely?
Are you solitary?
      Yes!
I have all the water in Minnesota
I have all the sunfish, the walleyes, the
Pike, the trout, the perch, the minnow and
The algae at my disposal.
      But still
I am in such wonderful solitude that
I don't like it.

Write me a letter Mr. Pheasant;
Pay me a visit, Madam Round Red Chested Robin
Respond to my cry, Mr. Coot
And also cry aloud for me, Mr. Goose,
      For
I will like to rule with all of you
      As
Minnesota State birds.

KWAME'S ALEX

WINTER:

Town of extremes
It was forty below yesterday
Today it is thirty below
And we feel warm
No school today
Why?
Why?! There is a snowstorm.
What has the storm left in its wake?
A majestic carpet of brilliantly white snow
So white
It's like God's own soul.

SPRING:

Exuberant life of recent greenery
Exuberant life of squirrels on a mating spree
Listen to the birds sing
The Robin is back
The Loon is back
The Goose is back
Even the coot is here.

Snow will melt in a piecemeal fashion
And the lucky farmers will plough
Their fields and sow,
The Soybeans
The Wheat
The Oats

The Potatoes

The Cucumbers

The Corn

Nature's Exuberant life?

Yes

All concocted in Alexandria Spring.

SUMMER:

Stay out and get a tan

But redhead don't stay out too long

Or you'll get sunburnt.

Land of extremes

It is 100°F today

Oh is it HOT!

Don't worry Alex,

We have our cool lakes

We will swim

Oh will we swim!

We will fish!

Oh will we fish!

We will waterski

Oh will we!

You better believe it

Come Come Come

Come to Wonderful

Alex

FALL:

What divine weather!

Indian summer you are my reference   .

What variation in majestic colors

Life is so short because alas, the beautifully
Colored leaves will all fall, all too soon.
But we still have hope because
God willing next year also
There will be fall
The Alfalfa
Thank you.

AFRICAN LEADERSHP (2)

Give way to traffic on your right!
Perpetual African leader, Mother Africa is

Tired of you and your rhetoric
Houphouet Boigny
Give way to traffic
Kenneth Kaunda
Give way
Hissene Habre
Give way
Gnasingbe Eyadema
Give way
Kanyon Doe
Give way
Kamuzu Banda
Give way
Musa Traore
Give way
Dauda Jawara
Give way
Mobutu Sese Seko
Give way
Siad Barre
Give way
Mengistu Haile Mariam
Give way,
Omar Bongo
Jerry Rawlings, Mugabe,

Give way
Muamar El Khaddafi
Give way
You are the
Cause of Africa's 'Humongous' problems
Leadership here is no Divine Ordinance nor Monarchy
Julius Nyerere, Leopold Senghor, Ahidjo
Realized it and gave way
Even Mighty Ronald had to constitutionally
Give way
Soon may be good Ole Margarette (the Iron Woman)
Will also
Give way.
Learn from History
Perpetual African Dictator.

AFRICAN FEAR

Hiroshima, Nagasaki
Why civilization?

Three Mile Island, Chernobyl, Fukushima
Why civilization?

Atomic Bomb, Nitrogen Bomb
Why civilization?

Napalm, chemical weapon
Why, oh why civilization?

You are going too far . . .
Really you are!

AFRICAN PRAYER

Some people want

them no get

Some people get

them no want

We, we want

We get

so

Help us God

Thanks

Amen.

KWAME MENDS' SAYING

THE GOODNESS OF MAN

IS

IMBUED IN

HIS

ABILITY TO

RESIST

TEMPTATION!

AFRICAN CONSERVATION

Why, oh why?
Just because of a piano key,
     A regal elephant must die.
Just because of Aphrodisia,
     A divinely solemn Rhino must die.
Just because of your encroachment,
Our lion, our giraffe, our gorilla
Our cheetah, our chimpanzee, our wildebeest
Our gnu, our impala, our zebra, our okapi . . . etc.,
     Alas, must die.

We kill what we eat
We eat all we kill
You don't even like elephant meat!
You just kill for fun and sport and money.

You decimated your bison
But that's OK with us
You decimated your bald eagle
But that's OK with us.
You decimated your California Condor, but that's OK with us
Where is the beautiful passenger pigeon I never saw?
We need our wildlife,
Stop poaching!

When will you stop killing the chinchillas for fur?
When will you stop killing the civet cat for perfume?
When will you stop killing the alligators for leather?

I hope you are skunked
When you kill the SKUNK!

AFRICAN MISSIONARY

You sit in your Benz
You sit in your Nissan Patrol
You sit in your Nissan Urvan
You ride on your Raleigh Bicycle
     and call yourself
        a
     Missionary.

Some Missionary indeed!
Why do you want the air conditioner?
Why do you want the cook?
Why do you want the washman?
Why do you want the watchman?
Why do you even want the garden boy?

Do you know how
St. Ignatius suffered?

Do you know the sacrifice
     of St. Damien?

Do you remember the sacrifice
    of St. Francis?

SACRIFICE African Missionary!
For the teaching of Christ
Is not a bed of roses
Know your kind,
    African Missionary!

AFRICAN MONEY

Money, who needs it?
Cedis, we need you!

Cedis don't be a devaluation slave.
We need you!

Cedis, why must I buy a small merchandise,
With countless thousands of you?

Are you an inflationary slave?

Former, former good cedi
Come back some day
For we really miss you!

AFRICAN LIFE

Full of opportunities, the African life
If you don't find them in

      Farming

      Fishing

      Mining

      Timber exploitation

      Construction

      Teaching, etc., etc.

          then

It's because you are lazy or coward,
Maybe you don't understand it

          for

If you did
You'd surely like to leave
Something
To immortalize your own
Very good name.

      Take note.

AFRICAN DECADENCE

Is it actually good
To watch or look at a
      Couple
      Cohabitating?
The white man thinks so
His videos prove it.

Yet he told us
Cover your breasts
Cover your nakedness
Yet she strips for money,
      beware
'Cos Ham knows it all too well.
He saw Noah's genitalia
      and
Bingo, the Black man
      is
Ham and a slave
White man thinks so, alas!

THE AFRICAN SAINT

Torn by war, drought, and famine,
I endure the dreadful pangs of hunger.

My body has become so dehydrated, so emaciated
The world looks on unconcerned.

And I slowly die by horrible hunger;
For no fault of mine.

Even the Christians fasted throughout the ages,
But none became so cadaverous like me.

Even the Muslims fasted throughout the ages,
But none became so skeletal like me.

    I, the Ethiopian child,
    I, the Sudanese child,
    I, the Somalian child,
    I, the Angolan child etc.

Will die quietly, unnoticed.
I know God has made me a saint
If the Pope doesn't.

AFRICAN HYGIENE

We won't just splash ourselves with musk.
We won't just splash ourselves with civet.

We won't use the man-made deodorant.
We won't use the cologne.
Yet:
We will take our baths twice a day.
And smell as God gave us: natural smell.

We will always shower and not just douche;
So that even our underarm and genital whiff
Is surely a pheromonal and nasal sense delight!

AFRICAN ANECDOTES

1. Everyone has problems
    Everyone has some joys
    Let us use the joys while they last, to overshadow our problems.

2. Our problems won't go away until
    We come together to solve them.

3. What we consider as problems might not be problems at all.
    If you think you have a problem, look at the next person. He might
    be languishing inside with a bigger problem and wishing that he
    had yours.

4. We begin to experience problems when we are afraid to open up.
    If we open up, I believe for a fact that these problems will go away
    instantly.

5. At the time of great joy,
    Let us look back at the great suffering and tribulations we've been
    through. Then our joy will be maximized.

6. Seriousness is the problem that lets
    One close his eyes for good. Alas, life,
    Shouldn't be wasted even if it's a mouse's.

7. There is hope for everybody who has life.

8. Let us believe and trust our Creator
   Who takes away our sorrows. For He will definitely replace it with joy.

9. We cry at sorrowful times for nothing.
   We should actually laugh at these sorrows
   And cry when we are happy because
   Things that make us happy are actually short-lived

10. Mary's words magnified the Lord
    But she was the mother of all sorrows
    At the Death of her son.

After the torture, the mental strain, the assault, the blood, lack of sleep, the waiting in the hospital for five hours with nobody caring or coming to see me. Finally, I am free as a bird. Now I can see clearly after the hurricane. All the destructions are visible now, but there is a coolness after the raging abated.

Stephen Kwame Mends

Author and author of AN AFRICAN LIVING WITH

DEPRESSION IN AMERICA with the pseudonym Stephen Kwame.

This is my lovely wife Irene Abeh Afriyie Mends

An excellent help in many times of trials and tribulations

These are Mr. And Mrs. Walt Salt,

my first American Father and Mother from Alexandria Minnesota

These are Mr. and Mrs Ercel Aga, my second American father and mother.

They are deceased but never will I forget them.

They were from Alexandria Minnesota.

Dr. and Mrs. Loren and Ruth Halvorson of Minneapolis Minnesota.
They have helped me a lot both spiritually and financially.